AUTUMN REBEL

THE WYTH COURTS BOOK 4

JULIANA HAYGERT

COPYRIGHT

This book is a work of fiction. Names, characters, places, and incidents either are products of the author's imagination or are used fictitiously. Any resemblance to actual persons, living or dead, events, or locales is entirely coincidental.

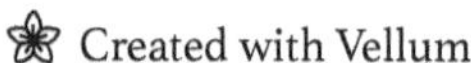 Created with Vellum

THE VAMPIRE HUNT

I have an exclusive novella set in the **RITE WORLD** that is just for my newsletter subscribers!

Click here to sign-up and receive your book!

THE VAMPIRE HUNT
A Rite World Novella

Norah is a demon hunter, one of the best graduated from the Blackthorn Hunters Academy. When she's sent to investigate a case concerning demons in a small town, she runs into a very arrogant vampire. Her first instinct is to kill him, after all, he's a supernatural and demon hunters are taught to end all evil.

Cain is a vampire prince. Because of his status, he's in charge of making sure humans don't find out about his kind. During a routine investigation, he bumps into a very sexy demon hunter and he wonders what she's doing on his way.

However, the case grows much bigger for Norah and Cain to handle alone. To find the truth and win this battle, the vampire and the demon hunter will have to hunt together —without killing each other.

How well could this end?

AUTHOR'S NOTE

I HOPE you enjoy reading *Autumn Rebel*!

DON'T FORGET to sign up for my Newsletter to find out about new releases, cover reveals, giveaways, and more!

If you want to see exclusive teasers, help me decide on covers, read excerpts, talk about books, etc, join my reader group on Facebook: Juliana's Club!

1

RED

EVEN THOUGH THE night was cold, the spiced wine was warm, and that kept the male fae going. I brought my cup to my lips, but stopped midway when the Winter fae clipped the chin of the Autumn fae with his fist.

The Winter fae cheered.

I groaned, drank the rest of the wine in my cup, and discarded it on the snow. "Come on, Lennox!" I yelled over the cheering.

Lennox threw me a heated glared before ducking under the Winter fae's arm and landing a hard elbow on the fae's back. His opponent lost his footing and landed face-first in the snow.

"Is this better?" Lennox asked, his voice high pitched.

I didn't have time to answer him as the other fae shot up and charged him, resuming the fight.

I looked around, searching for the young page who was serving drinks. I caught sight of him on the other side of the improvised ring, filling the cups of the other fae. Eventually, he would return this way. Meanwhile, I clutched the fur-lined cloak I had brought and tried to stay warm.

Whose idea was it to go traveling to other courts and offer them my services? Oh, yeah, mine. If I was here, suffering in the cold air of the Winter Court, it was my rusting fault.

But I couldn't deny that after a handful of days here, it was easy to get used to the cold and the snow. And the fae. The soldiers welcomed Lennox and me, and even invited us to two of these games. Every few days, they constructed a makeshift ring behind the barracks, where the noise wouldn't be heard from the castle, and fought among themselves. The only rule was no magic or weapons, only fists and your own strength. Bets ran freely with each match, but the money didn't seem to matter. The main thing was the camaraderie and the fun.

Things I hadn't encountered in a long time.

The first night they invited Lennox and me for the fights, I was skeptical. We were here as guests of the Winter King. I didn't want to sneak around and do something we shouldn't. But they assured me King Cadewyn—or Cade to his friends—knew about the fights, and even showed up once in a while to fight too.

I couldn't tell if that was true or not, but I chose to believe it was.

Lennox stopped playing and landed a rapid sequence of front kicks in the castle guard's chest that made him stumble back and lose his footing. Lennox advanced and brought up his fist in a beautiful uppercut. The guard went down.

Lennox lifted both fists to the air. "Yes!"

The soldiers around the ring groaned and exchanged coins. Only a few had bet on Lennox.

Sweaty but wearing a big grin, Lennox trudged to my side. The young page appeared and Lennox grabbed two cups of spiced wine. He offered one to me and brought the other to his lips, drinking it all in two big gulps.

When he was done, I handed my cup back to him. "It looks like you need this more than I do, captain."

Lennox didn't hesitate. He took my cup and emptied its contents. Then he reached to the side and fished his cloak from a bench lining the stone path—now mostly buried under the snow. He patted a hand over it, sweeping away the ice and snow that had clung to the fabric. He wrapped the cloak around his body and shivered.

"It was a good fight," he said. "This might be for sport, but it's different from the formal training."

"Different is good," I observed.

"Yes," he agreed. "The more we train with different styles and patterns, the better our fighting will be."

I nodded, but deep down, I wondered why we bothered. The last big fight in Wyth had been almost a year ago, when the witch Sanna had invaded the Sun City in the Summer Court. If it had depended on Crown Prince Lugh, we would have stayed away from that fight too, just like we stayed away when Cade had to deal with the Tabred invading and cursing his lands, and then when the

Spring Court had to fight their tyrant fake king, Vasant—alongside the witch, Sanna.

I had been fighting in the Autumn Court's army since I could hold a sword, and I would do anything for my kingdom, but I had grown tired of watching the disparities of Wyth from afar. Most of the other courts had united to fight together. Why couldn't we? Just because the former king thought our kingdom didn't need to depend on others? That we should be strong and efficient independently? Because he didn't want to have any debts to pay?

That had been many years ago. I had urged the crown prince to change his stance on the matter, but he wanted to follow his father's example. So, I remained quiet.

But at some point, I couldn't sit on my ass and watch anymore. Disobeying direct orders to stand down, I marched out of the Autumn Court and faced Sanna and the trolls with the other courts. And since then, I had barely stepped foot in my kingdom.

After helping at the Summer Court, I had gone to the Night Court and helped Prince Nix and Princess Amaya train a new crop of soldiers, and now here I was, at the Winter Court, helping General Kei with his soldiers. He wanted to train them in different styles and tactics than they were used to, and I was happy to oblige.

In the handful of days Lennox and I had been here, we had received many compliments from the generals and the king. I tried not letting that go to my head, but it felt great to be useful again.

Not that there wasn't much to do in the Autumn Court,

but I had always wanted—needed—a change of scenery. Now, I was finally getting one.

The fighting went on for two more rounds while the coins flowed, along with the wine and ale.

Then Xitan, one of the White Knights, walked to the middle of the makeshift ring and pointed his finger at me. "I challenge Prince Redlen for a fight."

A cheer erupted around the fae, and Lennox patted my shoulder. "I don't think you can get out of this one, Red."

Who said I wanted to?

I unclasped my cloak and pushed it into Lennox's arms. My sword had stayed back in my room, but I never left my dagger behind—I unfastened it from my belt and handed it to Lennox too. As I walked toward the ring, I rolled my shoulders and flexed my bare arms—I had been ready to fight. The soldiers whistled and cheered, eager to see a foreign prince getting his ass kicked.

As if I would allow that to happen.

I stepped into the ring and faced Xitan as he said, "Remember, my lord, no magic."

I nodded. When fighting, my instinct was to reach for my magic first—my power of the Autumn elements or shapeshifting into my fox form—but since arriving in the Winter Court, we had trained without any of it. It was a nice change of pace.

We positioned ourselves in combat stances—feet apart, fists raised, eyes locked in a defiant glare.

For a minute, we just stayed like that, facing each other, while the crowd around us exchanged bets. From the corner of my eye, I saw Lennox exchanging coins. He better be betting on me, or I would demote him to a castle guard when we got back to the Autumn Court.

If we got back to the Autumn Court.

When the chatting and movement reduced around us, someone yelled, "Fight!"

Xitan didn't waste time and came at me, his arms throwing punches left and right, forcing me to retreat backward and dodge in rapid succession. The worst part of fighting in this court wasn't how skilled the soldiers were; it was the rusting snow and ice. Even though the ring had been cleared of snow, a thin layer of sleet and ice remained, making it difficult to find footing. During the fights, I had seen many able fae fall because they slipped on the ice, and that had given their opponents an opening.

And they were all used to battling in these conditions. I wasn't.

I ground my heels on the ice as best as I could and held my ground when Xitan swiped a hook at my head. I ducked and landed a pretty uppercut to his stomach. The soldier gasped and stumbled back, losing his balance and almost falling back. He pressed a hand over his chest, inhaling deeply, but I didn't give him a chance to recover and come at me again. I charged headfirst and wrapped my arms around his midriff, taking him down. Again, he gasped for air. I allowed him two seconds to recover before straddling and raising my fist to his face.

"Surrender?" I asked.

One corner of his lips tugged up. "Never." In a flash, he scooped some of the snow accumulated at the edge of the ring and threw it at my eyes. I blinked, but in that one second, he acted. Taking advantage of my disorientation, Xitan flipped us and pressed my back on the cold ice. "Use your surroundings, prince." I groaned from the chill spreading through my body and from not being used to this scenery. Of course, the snow. "Surrender?" he asked, his fist lined with my head.

"Prince Redlen!" a voice echoed through the night.

The soldiers turned to the voice and stood at attention. Xitan clasped my arm and shot up, helping me stand beside him.

General Kei strode among the fae, coming toward me.

"Good evening, general." I ran a hand over my pants, patting off the ice and snow. "Were you looking for me?"

General Kei stopped at the edge of the makeshift ring. "Not me. King Cadewyn is asking for you."

I frowned. At this time of the night? "What is it?"

General Kei glanced around and as if he had issued an order, the soldiers dispersed and walked away. When no one else but Lennox and Xitan were within earshot, the general continued, "There's trouble at the border."

WHEN KEI SAID there was trouble at the border, I imagined it was the border with the Day Court or maybe the Dusk Court. I hadn't thought he meant south, where the Winter

Court met the Triad River, and beyond it, the Tywyll Forest.

The last I heard, Cade had joined forces with his mate, Amber, and the king of the Day Court. Together, they had conjured a magical barrier to keep the Tywyll Forest isolated forever. How could there be trouble now?

I met with the king in front of the White Castle, where he waited for me with a handful of his White Knights. The king and his knights shapeshifted into their wolf forms. General Kei and Xitan did the same. I glanced at Lennox and we shifted into our fox forms.

My fox was dark red, like my hair, and almost twice the size of Lennox's burnt-orange fox. Beside Cade's white wolf, my fox looked small, but what I lacked in size, I compensated for in agility and speed.

We rushed through the forest, our paws pounding the snow and ice covering the ground. I couldn't deny the Winter Court was a beautiful place, with all the eerie whiteness blanketing the earth and the ice wrapping around the trees, giving them a crystal-like shine. Shame it was a little too cold for my taste.

We slowed down when we arrived at one of the border outposts. Two guards emerged from it, and we shifted back to our fae form to talk to them.

The two guards bowed to their king.

"What's going on?" Cade asked. He had his long white hair falling down his back, and wore a fancy white fur cloak over his broad shoulders. "The report said there was movement outside the barrier."

"Yes, my king," one of the soldiers said. His name was Aimon. The other was Birch. I had seen them both before during training. "Right where the river narrows and becomes shallow. We saw shadows behind the magical barrier."

Cade glanced at me. "How about you and I go investigate?"

Before meeting Cade in front of the castle, I had made a quick stop at my room in the barracks—I had been offered a fancy guest chamber in the castle, but I had refused—to grab my armor and my sword.

Now, I placed a hand on the hilt of my sword, hanging from its scabbard at my hip, and nodded at the king. "I'm ready."

Lennox's brow slammed down and I knew what was going through his head. He had been my best friend since we were little kids. We had joined the army together, trained all our lives together, and when I advanced in rank, I arranged for him to serve with me. Most of our missions, most of our fights had been together, and he always got anxious when I left him behind. He had made a vow to protect me, and he couldn't keep that vow when he wasn't with me.

I looked at him and gave him a brief nod, assuring him that everything would be all right. Lennox pressed his lips in a tight line but didn't say anything.

Cade took the lead, and I followed. The two of us marched through the snow until it stopped at the river's bed.

"There," he said, pointing to a soft bend in the river, where it became a thin and shallow strip.

We approached the bend. I couldn't see the barrier, other than a murky glare in the distance, but I could feel its powerful magic brushing against me like a gentle wind.

I watched for movement or shadows behind the barrier but didn't see anything.

"Even if we see something, it's not like they can cross it, right?" I asked. "I mean, there's no way to break the barrier's magic."

Cade's brow was furrowed as he assessed the barrier for any weakness. "I don't know. How many times have we seen magic that was seemingly indestructible, and then something came and undid it?"

True. I hoped this wasn't the case.

"But—"

A shadow loomed behind the barrier and jumped through it. Cade lifted his hands and sent out a wave of ice, and I brought the wind, but it was too late.

The shadow caught us.

2

BLAIR

THE SWORD CAME for my head and I ducked, escaping the harsh strike that was sure to take me out of the fight.

"Oh my," someone whispered from the corner of the arena.

I rolled my eyes, but didn't spare half a second thinking about Jora and her worries. Because if I did, Sage would definitely take me down.

Sage stepped closer, jutting his blunt sword forward, the tip aimed directly at my chest. I parried his sword with mine and advanced a large stride at the same time, then landed a round kick to his open side.

"Good," he said, an easy smile overtaking his lips. The wrinkles around his eyes deepened. "Very good, my lady." The smile vanished and he moved. As fast as lightning, he stepped into my personal space, clasped a hand around my neck, and pulled me to him while pushing the tip of his sword into my stomach.

"Rust," I muttered.

"Oh my," Jora exclaimed again.

Chuckling, Sage let go of me and lowered his sword. "One of these days, she'll have a heart attack."

I ran a hand over my head, pushing back the strands that fell loose from my braid. "I already told her not to come to my training sessions, but she insists on it."

"I'm your handmaid, Lady Blair." She approached us, her face contorted into a glare. Her chubby cheeks were red with frustration, and her warm brown eyes were ice cold and locked on me. "It's my duty, my honor, to follow you wherever you go." She wrinkled her nose. "Even to this smelly place."

I smiled at her. The training grounds weren't that smelly. That, or I had grown used to it since I had spent a lot of time here since I was very young. I didn't understand how Jora wasn't used to it too, since she had been taking care of me for just as long.

"Another round, my lady?" Sage asked.

"No, no more rounds," Jora said before I could open my mouth. "We have to go, my lady; otherwise we'll be late for your visit."

Oh, rust. I had forgotten I had my biweekly visit this afternoon. I glanced down at my leather pants and vest, my red-brown boots and my thin beige tunic. "I don't think Lugh will mind seeing me like this."

Red spread over Jora's cheeks, indicating she was now not only frustrated, but a bit angry too. It was easy to bait her. "He might not mind seeing you like this, my lady, but the queen will." She grabbed my arm and tugged me toward the exit. "Now come, please."

I threw my practice sword to Sage. "I can't escape this."

"I know, my lady." He lowered his head. "I'll clean up too, and then meet you at the front gates."

"We leave in one hour!" Jora yelled at him, but her eyes faced forward, her steps sure, like a fae on a mission.

I wiggled my fingers at Sage, but didn't protest. I let my old friend take me to my chambers, bathe me, and pamper me.

PERRY, a royal guard, always came to escort me to the palace along with Jora and Sage. I once questioned why, thinking Jora and Sage were capable of riding with me the short distance from the nobles' district to the palace, but Lugh affirmed it wasn't only for security. It was to show the Autumn fae that I mattered.

It had been silly of me to question it, since I had been raised for this role, but I wasn't one to stay quiet in the back, and Lugh knew that.

Now, as the five of us—my mother, Bruna, had decided to join us—cut the capital in a slow gait, fae watched. Some stopped whatever they were doing when I passed and waved frantically, others stared with wonder in their eyes, and others eyed me with suspicion. I didn't let that bother me, though.

And it clearly didn't bother my mother.

"They adore you, Blair," she said with a smile. She waved at the fae as if she was the queen. I had to control the urge to roll my eyes at her. I loved my mother, and I knew she loved me. She had my best interest at heart, alongside with her ambition and desires for more.

My father was the polar opposite. He was a noble fae, a trusted advisor to the former king, who had been one of his best friends. But my father was a quiet and reclusive fae, and when the king died many years ago, he only closed up more. Now, he preferred staying in the shadows and watching his loved ones succeed from afar.

I liked to think I was a mix of the best parts of both my parents. The truth, though, was probably far from that.

I could let those thoughts consume me, or I could simply put one foot in front of the other and keep going. So, I glanced at the fae with a soft smile and let my eyes roam the capital. Masarn was a beautiful city with beige, white, and yellow buildings, topped by brown or red roofs, and yellow, orange, and red trees. The leaves fell on the cobblestone streets, creating a colorful carpet.

We turned the last corner leading to the palace, and as usual, I held my breath, taking in its magnificence. The Oren Palace stood tall against an orange valley, its brown stones solid and rough. Thin, long windows dotted its surface, and red vines grew along its sides. I had practically grown up inside this place, and yet, each time I came to visit, it felt like a stark shock. My parents were of noble birth and had raised me as their little princess, but our manor was still a far cry from the grandiose palace, and despite all my education and training and preparedness, I wasn't sure I would ever be truly ready for what was expected of me.

But I had gladly accepted the challenge. Like Lugh, what I cared about the most was the welfare of the Autumn Court and its fae.

Upon seeing us approach the palace, the guards opened the gates and bowed as we passed. Willow waited for us at the palace's entrance. I smiled as I dismounted and walked to her. With a wide smile, the young fae threw her arms around me.

I chuckled and embraced her tight.

About six months ago, King Varian of the Summer Court had sent a messenger, saying he had found a lost female fae in another realm. He had brought her back, but her memories were gone. Besides her name, Willow, she didn't remember how she got there or who her parents were. I went to retrieve her, sure I could bring her back to the Autumn Court and find her family with the snap of my fingers. Even though I had the full support of the royal family, I still hadn't found her family, or anyone who could claim her as their own.

Meanwhile, the royal family allowed her to stay in the palace, and treated her like a princess, which I thought she quite enjoyed. Princess Maize and Queen Aurelia had taken a liking to Willow, and I had started to wonder if they wished the young fae's family wasn't ever found.

"How have you been?" I looked down at her. She was still small and childlike, even though she was a teenager.

The many years she lived as a slave in the other realm had taken its toll.

"Good." She let go of me, but didn't step too far away. "I missed you."

I frowned. "I was here two weeks ago."

"I know, but you're always the kindest to me."

Together, we walked into the palace. My mother, Jora, and Sage followed behind us. "I thought you enjoyed the queen's and the princess's company."

Willow leaned closer. "I do, I really do, but they treat me as if I was a little girl. You don't."

I made a mental note to talk to the queen and the princess about it. Willow looked young, and she was a lot younger than us, yes, but she wasn't a child anymore.

The first few times I had come to the palace after my future title changed, I had been escorted by handmaids and pages and several guards, as if I didn't know my way around, or I was in danger. I hadn't complained. But as the years went on, I talked to Lugh about it, and thankfully, he heard me. Now, I moved freely around the palace with only Jora, Sage, and sometimes Perry following me around. However, I did notice the patrols and guards stationed in hallways and doors paid attention to my every step, as if they had been instructed to make sure I was okay.

This had been my life for years, and I still wasn't used to it.

Willow and I walked into the sunroom—a large beige and burnt-yellow room with sparkling brown floors, luscious handmade oak and cedar furniture, and red cushions. Windows covered most of the walls in the room, letting the sunlight in and warming the place.

Standing in the middle of the room, Queen Aurelia and Princess Maize smiled at me.

"My dear Blair," the queen said, her voice frail. She opened her thin arms to embrace me. "You look lovely."

"Thank you." I accepted her embrace, careful not to rumple her beautiful gown. Though she looked paler and weaker each time I came to visit, she still dressed for a ball every day. Her long, dark raven hair was carefully pulled into a knot at the nape of her neck, her delicate hands were covered with rings, and her wrists were adorned by bracelets. "How have you been?"

She pulled back and waved me off. "I'm old and uninteresting. Don't worry about me."

But I did worry. Everyone did. After the king died from the sea plague, Queen Aurelia had spiraled down a dark hole. No one had been able to rescue her from it. She withdrew from court affairs for many years. She left her kingdom unprotected and uncared for. Only recently she had started coming out for tea and walks again, but she still looked like she could snap and fall into that hole any minute.

Princess Maize was a younger, brighter copy of her mother. She too embraced me like a sister and asked me how I was doing. As usual, my mother fawned over the queen and the princess, throwing out more compliments than necessary and bowing her head about ten times per minute.

"Why don't we sit down?" Maize said, gesturing to the couches behind us.

"Of course." The queen was the first to sit in an armchair modeled after the throne in the main hall.

Princess Maize and Willow sat on a loveseat, and my mother took another armchair, a less opulent one, across from the queen. I was about to sit on another loveseat when someone else joined us.

I stood at attention. Princess Maize, my mother, and Willow rose from their seats. The only one who didn't move was Queen Aurelia.

"Good afternoon," Prince Lugh said. His dark brown eyes instantly found mine and he showed me a small smile. "Lady Blair."

"Hello, Your Highness." I curtsied, as I was taught to do, though I knew it irritated Lugh to no end.

My mother would have knelt on the floor and kissed his feet if he had asked that of her. For now, she settled for bowing low, showing her respect.

"Please, sit down, and be at ease." Lugh walked to my side, took my hand, and sat down with me. "I trust you've been well?"

"Yes," I answered. My eyes found our joined hands. I should have been used to this by now. Though it felt easy, it didn't bring butterflies to my stomach, or make my heart race. Which was a shame. He was handsome with auburn hair and a gentle smile. He was tall, and I knew for a fact he trained with the soldiers often, which gave him a fit body and muscled physique. I had seen court ladies and other nobles swooning over him. And yet, all I felt for him was a deep camaraderie. "How about you?"

Lugh sighed. "Well, yes, though very busy."

It was always the same answer. Sometimes he took me to his study and the council room and told me all that was happening in the kingdom. He knew the Autumn Court and its fae were important to me, and I cared about what was going on. He knew I wanted to help.

But for now, I observed.

Soon, that would change.

"You know," the queen started. She placed her folded hands on her knees and stared at Lugh and me. "I'm not getting any younger here. Though fae might live for many hundreds of years, I would rather not push my luck. Before I die, I want grandchildren."

I gulped.

"I agree, Your Majesty," my mother added. "Have you two decided on a date for the wedding?"

Lugh and I exchanged a glance.

When I was a little girl, I came a lot to the palace because of my father's position. He was part of the fae council who helped the king rule over the Autumn Court, but everything changed when I became a teenager and our parents agreed that Lugh and I would be betrothed. I continued coming to the palace after that, but while I came to play with the princes and the princess, I then went to visit my future husband.

Since then, my days had been spent on learning how to be the best wife a husband could have, and the best queen a kingdom could ask for.

No, Lugh and I had not decided on a date. To be honest, we barely talked about the wedding.

"We are in no rush, Mother," Lugh said, as polite as ever. I had seen Lugh lose his composure twice—the first when his father died, and the second when his brother left.

"You might not be, but I am," the queen said, her tone soft. Disappointed. "This kingdom could use a party."

"There are plenty of festivals and special dates being celebrated, Mother," Lugh said. "Choose one and throw a big party."

She shot him a glare.

My mother opened her mouth to add her voice to the marry-now chant Lugh and I heard often, but she closed it when General Barric walked into the sunroom.

The older fae bowed deeply. "My apologies, Your Majesty, but I need to speak with Prince Lugh."

The queen waved her hand, clearly annoyed with the interruption. Lugh patted my hand and went to meet the general. The two of them walked outside the room and talked in hushed tones. The queen, the princess, my mother, and Willow resumed talking about the wedding. How grand it would be, how many kingdoms they would invite and how they would show off, they even discussed ideas for decorations and food, but my attention was divided.

Though I couldn't hear what Lugh and the general were discussing, I could see half of Lugh's body from here, and he was as rigid as a board. His usually gentle demeanor changed completely and his jaw tightened.

Something was wrong.

A few minutes later, Lugh marched back into the room, but halted a couple of steps from the doorway. "I have grave news," he said. He glanced at me, and then at his mother.

The queen's brow curled down. "What is it?"

Lugh let out a long breath. "It seems we're about to be attacked."

"What do you mean?" I asked, my voice low. I wasn't sure, but somehow, I could guess his answer.

He nodded at me, confirming my thoughts. "The sea elves are back."

3

RED

CADE and I barely had time to take a step back and dodge the attack as two monsters—complete with dark gray skin, visible black veins, and snakelike red eyes—rushed us, their claws aiming at our heads, and their jagged teeth snapping toward our necks.

I forced the wind around us to funnel into the attackers. It didn't stop them, but it made them stumble to the side, giving Cade and me a breathing moment.

"What the rake?" Cade asked. He moved up his hands and ice formed around the monsters' legs, trapping them in place. The monsters fought against the ice but couldn't break free. Cade withdrew his sword and pressed the tip of the blade to the chest of the nearest monster. "What are you doing here? How did you cross the barrier?"

"W-we are running," the monster said, his voice clipped. This one was taller than the other monster, but slimmer, his limbs longer. His skin was also paler, but his red eyes were brighter. And there were a few patches of dark hair atop his head.

"Running from what?" Cade asked.

The two monsters exchanged an uneasy glance. "There have been fights among the tribes of the Tywyll Forest," the other one said. He had a nasty scar across his shoulder and neck. "It has been ... gory, to say the least."

"It's an endless war," the first one added. "The attacks come from nowhere, and everyone we know has fallen."

I frowned, almost pitying the monsters. Even though I knew they were greedy and nasty and plain vicious, they probably also had families and friends—in a way. If everyone this monster knew had fallen, then he was alone, and a part of me could sympathize with that.

"How did you cross the barrier?" I asked, bringing the questioning back to what we wanted to know.

Again, the two monsters exchanged glances. "My sister-in-law was half witch," the scarred one said. "She enchanted this before dying." He raised his hand. A simple gray stone rested in his palm.

Without lowering his sword, Cade reached for the stone. He hissed. "I can feel the magic in it." Cade looked at me, and I could read the question in his eyes.

How could a rusting witch cast a spell that would undo the combined magic of three powerful fae and a goddess? This witch had to be extremely powerful. If she hadn't died, I would be concerned right now.

Cade pocketed the rock. "Turn around and go back to your land. I don't care what is happening in there. Stay there and solve it. Or don't. But don't bring your problems into my land." He pushed the sword into the monster's chest, drawing a thin line of black blood. "Understood?"

I thought the monsters would argue, but thankfully, they didn't. Cade let go of his magic and the ice melted from their legs, freeing them. He went to the barrier and placed his hand on it—it opened, a tiny sliver. The two of them turned around, and with their shoulders slumped, they marched across the barrier once more. Cade retreated and the cut closed.

He patted the pocket of his pants. "I can't believe a stone like that could do this. Open and close the barrier."

"Let's hope there's no other witch like that in the Tywyll Forest," I said. "Make sure to keep this stone a secret and well hidden, and it should be fine."

Cade nodded at me, then let out a relieved sigh. "I had been so nervous we would discover something much bigger and worse than two runaway monsters ..." He rolled his shoulders. "You know what we need right now? A good drink. Let's have a nice dinner at the White Castle."

I smiled. "I will never say no to that."

***

FOR SOME REASON, this dinner was fancier and busier than the few others I had shared with Cade and Amber since arriving at the Winter Court. Besides the king and the queen, there were a few noble families in the grandiose dining hall, with its white walls, tall ceiling, heavy ice chandeliers, smooth white floors, and long, tall windows. The guests took seats across the long table. The general and some of the White Knights were also here.

Lennox and I sat on the other side of the long table— me at the head, and Lennox at my right side. On my left was Serena, a noble fae with beautiful cropped silver hair, who kept shooting me suggestive glances. Under the table, Lennox kicked my shins each time she munched on something and made little sounds, which should be reserved for bed only.

With the conversation loud, the laughter strident, the food and alcohol flowing, no one else heard her, or so I hoped. I didn't know much about her, but from the little I had seen, I could only imagine her reputation wasn't so pristine.

Neither was mine.

I let myself fall into her trap and leaned closer to her over the table. She started talking about her father, who had been a well-known White Knight under Cade's rule, then shifted the topic to me.

"I hear people calling you the rebel prince," she said almost purring. "I like rebels." She went on, but I didn't really hear much else of what she had to say. Every time I tried to focus on her mouth, on what I would have her do with it in an hour or so later, my mind took off in another direction, toward someone I promised myself I wouldn't think of again.

Who was I kidding?

I always thought of her. Even when I was busy with training, fighting, entertaining my men, she was always in the back of my mind, waiting for her turn, taunting me, making me miserable.

With a heavy sigh, I leaned back on my chair, my interest in the silver-haired fae gone. My hand rested on the dagger fastened to my belt, a habit I couldn't shake.

Suddenly, the conversation and sounds around the table stopped. Movement to my left caught my attention, and I turned to find out what had made everyone so quiet.

Mahaeru walked into the dining hall.

Everyone rose, including Cade, Amber, and I, and bowed to the goddess.

Her long, black hair fell like a curtain behind her back, and her black gown gave the impression that she was always ready for a funeral.

"Mahaeru," Amber said, taking a step closer. "What brings you here?"

"I have important news to deliver," the goddess said, her voice plain.

Cade braced himself. "What is it?"

Then, Mahaeru's eyes found mine. "Prince Redlen, I'm afraid you must go back home."

I frowned. "What for?"

"Sea elves' ships are approaching the coast."

My stomach dropped. No, this couldn't be. I glanced at Cade.

He nodded once at me. "You must go."

Lennox placed a hand on my shoulder. "Let's go."

I gulped the sudden anxiety brewing inside of me. After so many years away, it seemed I was going home.

THE PALACE WHIRLED WITH ACTIVITY.

The queen didn't receive the news well, and almost fainted. Libra, her handmaid, rushed into the sunroom and helped her to her chambers, where the palace's healer would be waiting for her. The princess and Willow followed the queen. My mother wanted to go with them, but she was sent home—she wasn't happy about that. Lugh had told me to go with my mother, but I had insisted on staying so I could help him.

While Lugh went to the barracks to talk to his soldiers and issue orders, I stayed back at the palace, where I instructed the staff on how to proceed—they all grew tense and agitated with the news. I also called on capital officials and asked Lugh to spare me a few soldiers so we could do something about Masarn. Though the capital was far from the coast, news of the incoming enemies would spread like wildfire, and agitation would follow. We had to contain the news, keep the fae calm, and assure them we had a plan.

I had studied the history of the Autumn Court, of all Wyth, for all my life, and I couldn't remember one time when the sea elves had invaded our kingdom and pushed inland. As far I as I knew, they had never been close to the capital, but of course, if it came to that, we would evacuate the capital. And for that, we needed preparations well ahead of time.

There was no rhyme or reason behind the sea elves' attacks. At least, no one had found one yet. All we knew was that their land was a miserable place, unsuitable for a quiet, peaceful life, and every so often they came to Wyth, to the Autumn Court specifically, wanting our lands.

King Linden had died after a battle with the sea elves many years ago. He had been successful in sending the enemies back to the sea—the ones who had survived the bloody battle—but he had succumbed after. It wasn't even because he had been injured by the blade of a sea elf. It had been because of the sea plague.

Some sea elves carried a virus that was inoffensive to them, but quite deadly to us. During the contact in battle, the virus spread. Most of the fae infected died.

When King Linden passed away, Queen Aurelia shut down, and Lugh, being the crown prince, assumed the kingdom's reign. In the beginning, he kept telling me it was temporary. Only until his mother recovered from the shock and sadness, but Queen Aurelia never recovered, and Lugh never backed down.

He was a king without a crown.

He didn't need one, though. The Autumn Court fae adored him, and his soldiers admired him. They would give their lives in an instant for their prince.

As would I.

That was why I had sent Jora home to grab my armor and my sword. When she came back, I went into one of the many washrooms in the palace, and changed my dress into leather pants, a tunic, and a vest, and attached the less bulky pieces of my armor—vambraces, rerebraces, and fauld. I also fastened my sword belt to the fauld. The rest, I kept inside the leather satchel so I could put them on later. Thankfully, my armor was much less complicated and heavy than most soldiers.

After getting ready, I went to the barracks with Jora and Sage trailing my steps. Perry had long ago left me to help get the palace ready for an attack.

Just where the path leading to the barracks ended before opening to the main training grounds, Lugh stood with General Barric and the other captains, talking in hushed tones. Behind them, a wave of soldiers rushed to ready for battle.

General Barric was the first to see me approaching. His eyes rounded and he bowed his head at me. "Lady Blair."

Lugh turned. His eyes found mine and a deep knot adorned his brows. "What are you doing?"

"I'm going with you," I said, deadpan.

The knot deepened. "No, you're not."

"That's not your choice."

With a huff, Lugh glanced at the fae behind him. "Excuse us for a moment."

The fae dipped their chins and walked away, out of earshot, and Lugh walked closer to me.

"I know you're going to the coast to see exactly what is happening, and I want to go with you." My voice remained calm, but firm. I wouldn't give him a chance to tell me no.

"Blair, I don't know what we'll encounter there. I can't risk having you with me."

"Like I said, this is not your choice," I repeated. "Why can the future king of the Autumn Court risk his neck, and the future queen can't? I want to protect this kingdom as much as you, and you know I can fight. I can defend myself, and even help, if it comes to it."

"Please, Blair, don't put me in this position."

"What position? Lugh, I'm not trying to undermine you. I'm trying to help. Please, let me help. Let the fae see how united we are, how we even fight our battles together." I fought the urge to put my hands on my hips—that would seem childish. "Besides, you can't really stop me. If I want, I'll grab my horse and follow you. I'm going either way. I just thought it would be easier if you agreed and let me go by your side."

Lugh groaned. He closed his eyes for a second, then looked at me again. "Fine," he said, his voice tight. He didn't seem pleased, but I was relieved. I thought I would have to argue with him longer. "But stay close to me. And at the first sign of trouble, I want you to flee. Got it?"

I wouldn't flee. I was going to help, but right now, I

would agree to anything. "Yes," I said, feeling a little exhilarated.

"All right." He glanced up and down at my armor. "I see you're ready. We're leaving in thirty minutes."

LUGH and I rode at the front of the long procession of soldiers. More had been called from the reserves situated across the kingdom, though the orders were to stay quiet about what was happening. The last thing we needed right now was panic spreading and creating chaos.

Thankfully, I had convinced Jora to stay back—having her pampering me while I was worried about a battle would be too much. But I didn't even try to talk to Sage about it. After all, protecting me was his life's job.

We rode for two days, as fast and with as few stops as the horses could take. A few elite soldiers went ahead of us in their fox forms, to scout and to set up camp, if we ended up needing one.

Finally, on the morning of the third day, we entered the wide road that led to one of the coast outposts—these outposts were small fortress with tall towers and strong walls. From there, soldiers watched the sea.

We passed through the camp as it took shape, and rode closer to the Mor Caer, the fortress from where the sea elves had been spotted this time. The tension in Lugh and the soldiers grew with each step our horses took.

"My prince," General Barric said, bringing his horse to Lugh's side.

"I know," Lugh said, his voice tight. His eyes were on the tall tower in the distance. The sun rose from the sea, illuminating the brown stone fortress and making the red vines growing over its side shine like blood. "The soldiers should have been back already."

I frowned. "The soldiers who went ahead."

"Yes," Lugh said. "I'm hoping they were detained by some quick matter, other than sea elves." Lugh raised his closed hand. The entire battalion stopped two seconds later. "And the scouts sent to the sea?"

"Those came back, your highness," General Barric informed him. "And they said the ships are a good way from the coast yet. If we wanted, we could make a stand on the beach to stop them."

Lugh's brow furrowed. "It has been days since we were informed of their approach, and they are still not here?"

"You think it's a trap?" I asked, thinking the same.

"I hope it isn't," he said. "I hope I'm mistaken and that for some reason the sea elves are still waiting on others and that's why they haven't come ashore."

"Your highness, the scouts said they ran the beach north and south for several miles and didn't find any foreign ships or vessels," the general assured him. "I don't think it's a trap."

"One can never be too careful." Lugh still stared at the tower, as if seeing something we didn't. "We'll go to Mor Caer's gates and check it out, but we can't risk taking all of my soldiers into the fortress." In case it was a trap—I could hear his unsaid words in my mind.

"I can go with a small group, your highness," General Barric said.

"I'll be going too," Lugh said.

"What?" I asked, incredulous. "If it is a trap, then you need to stay back."

"I agree with Lady Blair, my prince," General Barric said.

"I can't appear weak in front of our enemy." Lugh glanced from the general to me. "I'll be going with my soldiers."

I held tight to the reins in my hands. "Then I'm going with you."

OF COURSE, Lugh argued with me about going with him, but I didn't care. Once again, I reminded him, he had no say in what I did.

Sage was another one who complained about having to follow me into Mor Caer. As we approached the fortress, he grumbled that he would have preferred staying behind with the other soldiers, prepping our camp, a couple of miles back.

Lugh decided to take only a hundred soldiers with us. General Barric went ahead and called for the gates of Mor Caer to be opened. Slowly, the heavy wooden gates were pulled up and a line of Autumn soldiers appeared behind them—all dressed in dark brown and burgundy uniforms. The soldiers stepped back and allowed us to ride in the fortress.

Lugh glanced around, at the small open area between the tower and the first houses inside the fortress. "Where's your magistrate?"

"Here."

We turned to see a figure walking out of the tower, his uniform ill-fitting, and his face pale.

Too pale to be an Autumn fae.

Lugh and I realized what was happening instantly, but it was too late. We drew our swords as the gates closed behind us, cutting us off from half of the soldiers who were supposed to be here with us, and the soldiers who had opened the gates for us turned, their weapons at ready.

These weren't fae. These were sea elves. They had dressed in our clothes, dyed their hair so it was darker and looked like ours, and even stolen our weapons.

My stomach dropped.

If they were here, if they had taken the fortress, what had they done with the fae who were supposed to be here?

The soldiers who had entered with us formed a circle around Lugh and me. Sage stayed by my side, tension rolling off his body in waves.

The sea elf who had pretended to be the magistrate walked closer, as close as he could without being pierced with a blade should a soldier try to stab him, and smiled at us—a defiant grin that sent shivers up my arms.

"My dear prince," he said, his thick accent filled with

disdain and sarcasm. "I was starting to wonder if you would show up."

I glanced around as the sea elves revealed themselves. They were tall and slim, with long limbs and unusual fair skin, almost white in the sunlight. Their ears were pointed like ours, but longer, and their hair was white or light blond and cut in different styles. Their eyes, thin slits on their angular faces, were either yellow or light orange. Some of them sharpened their teeth, and I often wondered if they ate fae flesh too, or if those were for show.

"You seem to know who I am," Lugh said. "Perhaps I should know who you are?"

"But of course." The sea elf bowed his head. "I'm Ta'hun, one of the chiefs under our leader, Su'jin."

I didn't remember any Ta'hun from the history books I had read depicting the sea elves' invasions, but I did remember a Su'jin. He had been one of their chiefs in the last invasion, the one that killed the king.

Lugh's brow furrowed. He had realized that too. "I suppose there isn't anything I can offer you for your retreat."

Ta'hun shook his head. "We'll stop once we have claimed Wyth."

I clenched my hands into fists and clamped my mouth before I spoke up and created more problems. I wanted to ask them why they seemed so invested in taking our lands. Why they kept coming back, even though we defeated them every time. There had to be a reason. History books mentioned their own land was inhabitable, but the truth was, no one knew that for sure. We had never captured a sea elf alive who was willing to tell us the details of their land.

All we had were guesses.

"I thought you would say that," Lugh muttered. For a brief moment, his shoulders sagged, as if he was tired of this battle already, and it had barely started. Then, he straightened and faced Ta'hun. "You know we won't go down so easily." Lugh raised his hand and the soldiers around us readied themselves.

"Oh, I expect that, my prince." Ta'hun offered us another wicked grin. "But don't worry. This time, our plan won't fail, and soon, your Autumn Court will be ours."

"Not if—"

In the blink of an eye, Ta'hun grabbed a spear from one of the other sea elves and threw it at Lugh. It was so fast, so unexpected, no one had time to react. Before I realized what had happened, Lugh had a spear deep in his chest and he slid down his horse.

"Attack!" General Barric cried.

Shouts and the clank of metal echoed through the fortress, but my mind, my focus was locked on the crown prince. Pushing down my panic, I jumped from my horse and rushed to Lugh. Sage was beside me, and with his help, I grabbed Lugh's shoulders and eased him to the ground.

On my knees, I hovered over him, my eyes on the giant spear protruding from his chest and the copious amount of blood seeping from the wound.

"By the chilly wind," I muttered. My vision blurred with tears. I cupped the crown prince's face. "Lugh? Can you hear?"

"Blair," he whispered, his trembling hand reaching for me. His eyes blinked fast, as if he wanted to clear them up so he could see. "I'm ..." He coughed and blood dripped down his chin.

Oh, no, no.

The woosh of wind sounded over my head. In a flash, Sage was up and pushing back the blade that had come for my head. I dared glancing around and the pit of despair that had opened in my chest the moment Lugh fell only grew deeper.

Ta'hun and his sea elves were cutting through us like we were weeds. The fae soldiers on the other side of the gates were doing all they could to open it. When they were able to lift it up by a foot, they placed something underneath it, and a few slipped inside to help us.

But the bodies were piling up around us. They shouldn't come in; we had to get out.

When Sage knelt back beside me, I said, "Help me." I hooked my arm around Lugh's and tried hoisting him up.

"Lady Blair," Sage said, his tone grave.

"Don't Lady Blair me," I snapped. "Just help me."

"Blair," Lugh whispered. More blood came from his mouth. "Stop." He took my hand in his. "There's ... nothing you can do." He pushed his sword toward me. "Sage. Get her out of here."

"What? No!" I held Lugh's arms, but his head lolled

back and his eyes closed. His arms fell to his sides. I stared at him in utter horror. "No, no."

Ta'hun was right there, standing by Lugh's head. He smiled at me and swung his sword. I didn't move. I watched as the blade came for me. Suddenly, two pairs of arms took hold of me and pulled me back. I didn't see much of what happened next—only that somehow I was holding Lugh's sword and retreating from the fortress.

Leaving Lugh behind.

When I finally came to my senses, I was atop my horse, watching as the sea elves surrounded Lugh's body. Standing with a foot on top of Lugh's chest, Ta'hun smiled at us, teasing. Taunting.

"We have to go back for him," I said, taking the reins of my horse and turning him around. "We need to get his body back."

General Barric and Sage moved their horses so they were in my way.

"Please, Lady Blair," Sage said, his eyes the saddest I had seen them in the long time he had been my protector. "Listen to reason. There's nothing you can do for him now."

General Barric stared at me with his misty eyes. "Lady Blair, let me save you, at least. Please."

I stared at the fortress, at the sea elves.

If I went back, I was good as dead.

I knew they were right, but it was too rusting hard. I couldn't move. So, I didn't. In the end, Sage took my reins back and guided my horse away, because if it depended on me, I would either stay planted in that spot, or I would do something crazy.

As we put some distance between us and Mor Caer, the weight of what had happened crushed me. I didn't fight the tears. I welcomed them as I hunched over my horse and sobbed for our crown prince.

5

RED

I WAS on my way to the coast when I received a message from General Barric, asking me to go to the Oren Palace instead. I didn't understand why; there was no other explanation in the note, but since General Barric was the most decorated soldier of our army, and Lugh trusted him blindly, I didn't think much about it. I assumed Lugh had asked him to send me the message, so I changed my route and went to the capital.

Upon arriving, I noticed something was wrong right away. As Lennox and I crossed the outer gates with our horses, we saw soldiers with a black band tied on their left arms, and black strips of clothes hanging from store entrances and windows of houses.

Someone had died.

My first thought was my mother. Queen Aurelia had been sick with depression and sadness since my father died. Several times, I had believed she would either take her own life to join him, or she would let herself wither away, until only her body was left.

It had finally happened.

But I didn't wait to see. I approached one of the guards at the gate and asked him what was happening, who had died.

"I'm sorry, Prince Redlen," the guard said, his eyes to his feet. "We were instructed not to dispense any information, not even to you. You should go to the Oren Palace and see for yourself."

That didn't sit well with me.

Knowing I could be faster than a horse, I hopped off the mare I had borrowed from the Winter Court, shifted into my fox, and raced to the palace.

I hadn't come all the way from the Winter Court to here in my fox form because I would tire too fast and needed more rest than a horse would. But now ... now the distance was short, and the curiosity hurt.

Lennox also turned into his fox and followed me. We arrived at the palace and again no one told us what was happening, but everyone looked solemn and sad, all of them sporting the black bands around their left upper arm, or in full black clothing.

Once in the palace, I shifted back into my fae form. "Lugh? Mom?" I called in the grand entrance, my voice echoing through the tall and wide hallways.

General Barric appeared from a side corridor. "This way, Prince Redlen." He gestured for me to follow him. I held my tongue as a hundred questions assaulted my chest and followed him into the Maple Courtyard—a burnt orange and soft red garden with thin trees and full bushes, brown stone benches, and a large fire pit in the center.

My mother, my sister holding the hand of a younger female fae I didn't know, and Blair stood around the fire pit. They were all wearing black gowns and sniffed in almost synchronicity.

Realization clawed at me as I made my way to them. My eyes found the sword atop the fire pit, confirming my fear. My knees buckled, and I almost fell to the ground. "Lugh," I whispered.

Blair reached for me and clasped her hands around my arm, steadying me. Even though I was keenly aware of her touch, I couldn't peel my gaze from the fire, from the sword growing red in it.

"I'm so sorry," Blair whispered.

Finally, I snapped and jerked away from her touch. "What the rake happened?"

A tear rolled down Blair's fair face. My mother let out a loud sob and pressed a hand to her chest.

"Mother!" Maize yelled, turning to our mother and holding her.

Blair turned to the queen and helped Maize as my mother fainted. I should have stepped up and helped, but my mind was a jumble of thoughts and questions, and my chest was imploding with too many feelings. I couldn't do anything. I couldn't *move*.

My mother's and my sister's handmaids came forward

and helped them. They escorted my mother out, and my sister and the young fae followed.

Though I knew Lennox, General Barric, Sage, and Jora were at the courtyard entrance, I felt like I was left alone with Blair and the sword in the fire pit.

I gulped hard and walked closer to the fire pit. I wanted to reach out and touch the sword, as if I could touch my brother, as if I could save him of whatever fate had him.

"What happened?" I asked again, this time in a low voice.

Blair inhaled deeply. "The sea elves set a trap for us in Mor Caer. We went in, thinking they were still out at sea."

I stared at her. "*You* went with him?"

"They killed Lugh," she said, not answering my question, probably on purpose. "I tried to take his body, but there were too many of them." Her voice broke, and she wiped another tear from her face. "I could only take his sword before Sage and General Barric dragged me out of there."

More information, more feelings I could barely control. I had lost my brother, and I couldn't believe Blair had been there. She could have been lost too.

I fell to my knees, my shoulders heavy. "I should have been there."

A soft hand landed on my shoulder, and I struggled to know what to do. I wanted to both take her hand and pull her closer, and I wanted to jump away, to be as far as I could from her.

She was my brother's betrothed. The brother who was

now dead.

This knowledge choked me. It squeezed my chest until it was too hard to breathe.

Besides the pain of losing my older brother, there were other problems we needed to solve soon.

I inhaled deeply and pushed up to my feet. "We still have a battle to fight, and despite having lost our crown prince, we need to show them we're strong and united."

Blair's hand dropped and her gaze along with it. A knot appeared between her delicate brows when she saw the dagger secured to my waist.

"I—" I opened my mouth to blurt out some excuse, but a new voice saved me.

"The rebel prince has returned." Blair and I turned to see Mahaeru walking into the courtyard from one of the many entrances. I didn't care about that nickname, since it fit me well; after all, I had abandoned the royal life long ago, and for many years, I even had been away from the Autumn Court, but coming from Mahaeru's mouth, it seemed more like an insult.

I groaned. "Oh, you again."

"There's no time to mourn," she said casually, as if she was simply stating the menu for supper.

"You knew this would happen, didn't you?" The goddesses were sacred and divine creatures to be loved, feared, and worshipped. But right now, I despised them. "Couldn't you have opened a portal and sent me here? So I could have been at his side during the trap? So I could save him?"

"Shh," Blair whispered, punching my arm. "Don't talk like that to a goddess."

"This is her doing," I barked, glaring at Mahaeru.

"It wouldn't have made any difference," the goddess said. She halted across the fire pit and looked at us with her hooded black eyes. "Even if you had been by his side, he would still have succumbed, and you would still blame yourself for not being able to save him. The only difference is that if you had been there, you would have lost your mind during the battle, and someone else would have tried to reason with you, someone you care for. And she would have died trying to save you."

Her gaze landed on Blair.

Oh, rust.

I gritted my teeth. "What are you doing now, then?"

The goddess's chin lifted an inch. "I came to remind you, you're the crown prince now."

My stomach dropped. I had considered so many things that became a bigger problem with my brother's death ... the war against the sea elves, the fact that now Blair was betrothed-less, and that we didn't have a crown prince anymore. But I had forgotten who was next in line.

Me.

"I can't," I said, my voice barely a whisper. I shook my head. The Autumn Court was a great kingdom, and it deserved someone better than me. "I can't be crown prince. Give the title to Maize, or even Blair." I gestured to her. Though I hadn't seen her in years, I had heard all about how great she was, how she had grown into her future queen role, how the fae adored her, and how fair and beautiful she had become. I knew none of those were lies. Blair would make a fine queen, with or without a king.

She gasped. "I'm not of royal blood. This is your duty."

I shook my head again. "I don't want it."

"Prince Redlen—"

I pointed a finger to Mahaeru, shutting her up. "Don't! I don't care about that, not now." I ran my hand through my hair and shifted my weight. "I just ... let me send these rusting sea elves back to where they came from, *then* we can talk about this subject. Until then, I don't want to hear another word."

"Pushing it aside won't make it go away," Mahaeru said. "The responsibility is still yours."

I clenched my fists. Would it be wrong to hit a goddess? Could I? I bet she would see me coming and strike me down before I could blink. But would she strike me down now that I was the heir of the Autumn Court?

"Whatever," I grumbled. "Right now, my focus will be on our enemies." I turned my back to the goddess and walked to where Lennox, General Barric, and Sage stood like statues, near one of the entrances. I nodded at the general. "We leave for the coast in an hour."

MY FIRST STOP was Lugh's chambers. I hadn't seen my brother in so long, I needed to know he was still the same serious and dedicated fae he used to be when we were younger. I walked around, taking in the details. Though his bed was made and everything was clean, his mess hadn't been touched. There was a pitcher of water beside his bed. His robe was lying on the armchair beside the nightstand. And open books and scrolls took over every inch of the place. Some of them were for pleasure, but most were war strategies and history books detailing what went wrong and where, and how to fix it. A notebook and pen and ink rested on the desk on the other side of the room, as if Lugh had stopped writing mid-sentence. Knowing my brother, he had been studying to be the best king the Autumn Court had ever seen.

If given the chance, I knew he would have been the best.

And now this duty fell on my shoulders like a heavy cloak, pulling me down and suffocating me. No, I wouldn't think of this. I wouldn't even dare go there. First, I had to deal with the sea elves. Only after that would I think and talk about what happened to me now that Lugh was de—

I inhaled deeply. I still couldn't believe it.

My older brother was dead.

I pressed a hand to my chest as if that could ease the pain.

Next, I stopped at my chambers. They were similar to Lugh's and Maize's, with a sitting room, then the bedroom at the back. While Lugh's looked like it was still inhabited, mine looked like a museum. There was no dust or dirty spots. The bed was also made and ready, but there was nothing else. No details, no paintings, no books, no decorations that were mine. I hadn't slept here in so long.

Then, I visited my mother in her chambers.

"The healer just left," Maize informed me as I approached the bed.

Queen Aurelia was lying in bed, a plethora of pillows propping her back up, but she wasn't sleeping. She was looking out the window, and not seeing anything.

Once upon a time, my mother had been a happy and energetic queen, the most perfect mate my father could have. Together, they ruled the kingdom with firm but loving hands.

Until he died and left her alone. Then she became a shell.

I stopped across the bed from my sister. "Is it just shock?"

Maize nodded. "Losing father was too much for her. Now losing Lugh is breaking her all over again. She hasn't been coherent since Blair came back with his sword."

Blair ...

I didn't want to think about her yet. No, I didn't have the head space for that.

Rust, so many things I was pushing back for later.

"How are you holding up?" I asked, looking at my sister. When we were younger, she had been spoiled, a brat, but it seemed time had done her well. She had grown into a beautiful fae with a firm stance, and she was by our mother's side when she needed her the most.

Maize's brown eyes filled with tears. "I'm breaking on

the inside, but I won't let that drag me under. I know we have to be stronger for her." She nodded her chin toward our mother. "For our kingdom." She wiped at her eyes before the tears fell. "Did you realize you're now the cro—"

I raised my hand. "No, don't go there. I don't want to think about that. One problem at a time."

She nodded. "Always the rebel prince. But I understand." She brushed a strand of her light orange hair aside and inhaled deeply. "And how are *you* doing?"

I scoffed. "Don't you know me? I'm locking my feelings away and just acting, doing what I have to."

"Even when it comes to Blair?"

I frowned. Maize was the youngest of all of us when Blair got betrothed to Lugh, but even she wasn't blind. Sometimes I think that even our parents had seen what was happening, and for some reason, they had been against it.

"Even that," I said between gritted teeth. I raked my brain for some other safer subject, and found one. "Who's the young fae? The one who was in the courtyard with you?"

"Oh, Willow," Maize said. "Remember King Varian of the Summer Court and Layla were stuck in that nameless realm? She was there too. After Varian and Layla came back, they went there again to rescue Willow. Varian contacted us, so we could help find Willow's family. We've brought her here, but so far, we have had no luck finding her family."

I remembered how close she was to my mother, and

how she held Maize's hand. "But it seems she found one already."

A small smile spread over Maize's lips. "Well, I'll be honest. Yes, I want her to find her family, but I don't want her to leave us. I'm growing fond of her. And mother is too." I nodded. Though I didn't know Willow, I could see she had brought some light and happiness to this household.

"Where's Willow now?"

"I don't like her seeing mother this way," Maize said, her voice grim. "Willow suffered a lot already, and I can feel how seeing mother unraveling distresses her. I sent her to her bedroom with her handmaid. Hopefully, mother will be fine by suppertime." She paused.

"You're doing good, Maize." The words tumbled out of my mouth before I even thought of them. But it was true. My little sister was surprising me.

Perhaps Mahaeru was wrong. The title didn't have to be mine. Perhaps Maize would be a good queen.

My sister straightened, her eyes falling on the sword hanging by my waist. "Are you leaving soon?"

"As soon as I say goodbye to you two, and get my things ready." I sat down on the mattress beside my mother and touched her hand. "Mother?"

Slowly, she turned her head to me. Her eyes rounded when she saw me. "Redlen, you're here!"

I forced a smile. "Yes, Mother, I am."

"I missed you so much," she said, turning her hand so

it would fit in mine. "Have you seen Lugh yet? I'm sure he'll love to know you're here."

"I—" I swallowed hard. "I'll talk to him later."

Maize sniffed and turned away, hiding new tears.

"Good, good." My mother patted my hand with her frail one. "I'll ask Libra to inform the cook we'll have a special banquet tonight. To celebrate we're all together again."

"That would be great," I said, going along with her. Arguing about the reality would only bring more stress and shock to her.

Maize turned and took mother's hand from mine. "Mother, Redlen is busy with army matters. He needs to go now, but he'll be back soon."

"Oh, of course," my mother said. "I'll let you go. I'll even lie down here a little." She pulled one of the pillows from her back, and Maize helped her down. "I'm tired. I'll nap until the time for the banquet."

She had certainly lost it. "Sure, Mother," I said, my voice heavy with agony. Maize glanced at me and I mouthed, "Thank you." She dipped her chin once, then returned her attention to our mother.

The queen wasn't this bad when I first left the Autumn Court. It broke my heart to see how far she had fallen, and the reality that she might never recover.

Wishing I could do more, wishing I could fix everything, I turned and marched out of my mother's chambers.

There was one thing I could do now: kill some rusting sea elves.

6

BLAIR

I watched as Red marched out of the courtyard. Lennox and General Barric promptly followed him, while Sage and Jora stayed back, watching me. Jora's eyes met mine, pity stamped on her face, before she lowered her gaze.

Though I didn't share half of my thoughts with her, she knew my true feelings. Despite trying to maintain my composure, I was disconcerted. My poor heart beat fast, in a way that scared me. I hadn't seen Red in years, and his effect on me hadn't lessened. In fact, it had increased.

He had grown; he was a couple of inches taller, his shoulders were broader, his arms were thicker. His leather armor accented every curve and dip of his hard body. His hazel eyes gleamed golden, and his hair, seemingly black in the shade, shone a dark red in the faint light of the sun. Short stubble covered his proud chin and sharp jawline.

He had been handsome when younger. Now, he was perfection.

"I know what you're thinking," the goddess said.

Heat covered my cheeks, and I turned to face her. How could I have forgotten she was here? And, by the fallen leaves, I hoped she didn't know what I was thinking!

"What do you mean?"

"You want to go to the coast with him."

That was absolutely true. "I could convince Lugh, but I'm not sure I can convince Red." He always had a more volatile personality. He could be fair and loyal and fun, but when something didn't go his way, he grew angry and over-reacted. Only the gods knew if he had changed. "He might throw me in the dungeon for bringing it up."

"He will throw a fit, but you'll convince him." She paused, her dark eyes fixed on mine. Her brows curled down. "Go. You have to. He'll need you."

MAHAERU DIDN'T HAVE to tell me twice. Once again, I sent Jora to fetch my armor and sword, while Sage secured a position with the soldiers marching to the coast, and I checked on the queen, Maize, and Willow.

As soon as she heard the news, Queen Aurelia collapsed. After that, it was a toss between shock, denial, and forgetfulness. Maize and Willow didn't leave her side while I prepared a quiet ceremony in the courtyard with Jora and two other palace workers.

Though my heart was breaking, I fell into battle mode. When we fled the fortress, General Barric had left a captain and ninety percent of our soldiers there to hold the sea elves back, in case they decided to pursue us or advance. They had already taken Mor Caer; we couldn't let them take anymore.

They had taken our crown prince.

My betrothed.

I had always loved Lugh, but not as a lover. He had been a childhood friend, then he had become a partner. We respected and loved each other as friends and companions. Deep down, I hoped that once we were married, we would eventually fall in love, though I wasn't sure that would be enough to snap the mating bond into place.

Now, I would never find out.

I pushed away these tormenting thoughts and feelings and focused on what had to be done at this moment. Red was right. We could argue about who would take the crown later.

Now, we had sea elves to kill.

After making sure my armor was secured, and I had everything I needed for yet another excursion to the coast, I went to the palace's front gate, where I knew Red was waiting for the soldiers. General Barric, Captain Runt, Lennox, and Sage were talking to him, while more and more soldiers arrived from the barracks and from the city. Lugh had put out a call for any trained fae who could fight the sea elves. Only a few had trickled in, but once news of his death had gotten out, the fae hadn't stopped arriving. They came from all corners of the kingdom to defend our land and honor their fallen ruler.

I was proud of them.

It was time to make Lugh proud.

I braced myself as I walked down the palace's front stairs. Red turned, his eyes finding mine. I sucked in a sharp breath and fought the urge to place a hand over my weak heart.

The sunlight hit him just right, giving his hair that dark red shine, and his hazel eyes seemed almost golden from here. His armor was brown and burgundy, like the other soldiers', but his had more details and embroidery, even more than the general's—Red was supposed to be Lugh's commander, even if he hadn't been home in years. It matched Lugh's armor; I knew that. Red pressed his lips tight, and his jaw popped. I knew what was coming. I was ready for it.

He met me halfway. "What the rust do you think you're doing?"

I halted before him and lifted my chin. "You know what I'm doing."

"Sage said you would want to come, but I thought he was joking." Red shook his head. "I don't care if you know how to fight, if you can defend yourself. You're not coming."

I took a step closer, invading his personal space, and looked deeply into his eyes. Red stiffened. "I said this to Lugh a week ago, and I'm going to say to you. You're not my owner. You don't order me around. You can tell me not to come; it doesn't matter. I'm coming anyway, even if I have to go by myself."

Red narrowed his eyes and a vein ticked in his temple. "Do I have to lock you in a bedroom?"

I leaned even closer. His eyes rounded. "I would like to see you try," I whispered.

Taking advantage of his shock, I walked around him and went to meet the rest of the fae. They all greeted me as we mounted. Red didn't talk to me as we guided our horses out of the gates and out of the capital. In fact, he avoided me most of the trip to the coast.

That hurt more than I would like to admit.

7

RED

"Are you going to keep avoiding her?"

I groaned. If we weren't on horseback, I would have leapt at Lennox and punched his nose for stoking the fire raging inside me.

"Just ... shut up," I said, trying to focus on the road. I glanced ahead at the orange glow the setting sun cast over the road. It was our second day riding to the coast. We pushed the horses as fast as we could for as long as we could, and gave them frequent breaks.

Lennox and I pulled up the front, keeping everyone's pace up. And all the while, Blair rode at the back of the party, with Sage beside her. At night, when we stopped, she camped several yards away from us. That had bothered me. Instead of sleeping, I tossed and turned on my mat, thinking sea elves or wild animals would attack her, and I would be too late to save her.

Just like I had been too late to save Lugh.

My heart squeezed, and Mahaeru's words haunted me.

She would have died trying to save you.

Losing Lugh was already too much for me. If I had lost Blair too ... I couldn't think of that.

"You know you'll have to face her at some point, right?" Lennox asked. Another jab at my gut. Only he could talk to me like that. Lennox was my oldest friend, my only confidant, my right arm. He knew everything about me, even the feelings I tried to hide from myself.

Especially my feelings for Blair.

"I already faced her," I said, my voice tight. "A handful of times since we arrived."

"No, no." Lennox shook his wild red mane. "At some point, you'll have to sit down and talk to her."

"Why? There's nothing to talk about." I frowned. There were many things to talk about, and the main one right now was what would happen to her after we sent the sea elves away. She had been betrothed to my brother for so long, she had been preparing to be queen for years, and now my brother was dead. "Can we change subjects?"

"But it's so much fun to tease you about your first love." Lennox flashed me a wide smile. I wanted to hit him more and more by the second. "Well, your only love, right?"

"Drop it," I snarled through gritted teeth.

"Only when I can see it doesn't bother you anymore."

"Rust you." I yanked at my horse's reins and turned him around.

Every couple of hours, I rode around the party, making sure all the soldiers were well and all the horses were keeping up nicely. It wasn't a big party, as most soldiers were already at the camp Lugh had set up before the battle at Mor Caer. But it was still a sizable group that could make all the difference in the battle ahead.

I also checked on Blair, even though I didn't get too close.

This time, though, I wanted to prove Lennox wrong. I wanted to show him—me—that she didn't have the same effect on me as she had when we were younger.

When we thought we were in love.

So, after making sure everyone was all right, I brought my horse to the end of the group, and instead of rounding the back as I had done every other time I had come this way, I kept into step with her.

Blair saw me coming and stiffened instantly, and Sage fell back several lengths, giving us privacy.

I guided my horse to stay in line with hers, and for a couple of minutes, we rode side by side in tense silence.

"I'm sorry," she whispered.

That took me by surprise. I glanced at her, and she took my breath away. Her long red hair was tied in a loose braid behind her back, the profile of her face as she stared forward showed me her thin nose and the pucker of her red lips. Her golden skin was smooth, and her pointed ears were smaller and more delicate than most.

She looked fierce in her dark brown armor, and yet her expression, her beauty gave her an air of gracefulness that wrenched at my heart.

I looked away before I surrendered my soul to her.

"For Lugh," she said, her tone still low. "He was your older brother, your friend. I remember when we were little that you looked up to him for everything." She inhaled deeply. "And now he's gone, and I couldn't save him."

At that, I looked at her again. "It wasn't your fault." That was my burden to carry.

She sniffed and turned her amber eyes to me. They gleamed with unshed tears. "I know, but I was right there. I feel like I could have done more."

"You heard Mahaeru. There was nothing we could have done."

I knew she had understood what the goddess had said about losing someone else in that battle if I had been there. Blair had always been brilliant and smart. She didn't need us to spell it out for her.

"Still, this is something I'll carry with me forever."

I nodded; even though Mahaeru told me I couldn't have saved Lugh, I would forever think I could have done something different to change his fate. "Me too," I whispered.

Blair wiped the tears away. "So, what are your plans?"

I hesitated. Once upon a time, Blair had been closer to me than Lennox ever was. She had been my best friend, my supporter, and my lover. It had been brief, but it had been intense, and it had meant everything to me.

"I don't have any plans yet," I confessed. "I'm waiting to get there, assess the situation, gather with the generals and captains, and then I'll make a plan."

She nodded. "It makes sense."

"Hopefully, it'll all be over fast," I muttered, more like a prayer than anything else.

We rode in silence for a few minutes, until she jerked her chin toward me. "I see you still have the dagger."

I put a hand over the dagger fastened to my belt. The beautiful blade was hidden in a scabbard, but the hilt gave it away. "I do," I said, feeling like I was a teenager again.

"I thought you would have gotten rid of it." A sharp edge entered her words.

"It's a great weapon," I blurted. "It would be a shame to throw it away."

Truth be told, I had tried getting rid of the dagger after I left, but I couldn't. Blair had given it to me for my birthday a handful of weeks before our world changed forever. It was my most precious possession. I carried it with me wherever I went. That and ... I patted my chest, right where a hidden pocket lined the inside of my vest. Her letter was neatly folded there—the only letter she sent me after I left. In the first few months, I read it every day. Now, I didn't anymore as I knew the words by heart. I liked to have it close to me. But she didn't need to know about it.

In the distance, a horse galloped down the length of the group, coming straight at us. I stiffened, but recognized Afal, the soldier I had sent ahead to tell the soldiers at the camp that we were coming, and ask for a report of the situation.

My first instinct was to ride away from Blair, but for some reason, I wanted to stay by her side.

Afal slowed his horse as he approached us. "Prince

Redlen," he said, turning his horse to fall into step by our side. "Lady Blair." He bowed his head to her.

"Tell me," I urged, growing tense.

"The sea elves have fully arrived, my prince," Afal said. "Their ships are offshore, and their tents are spread out on the beach for miles in both directions. But they have not attacked our soldiers since the battle at the fortress."

"Good," I muttered. Well, not good that our enemies were taking over our coast, but good that there had been no more deaths. "Thank you."

Afal dipped his chin, then joined the other soldiers.

"Are you okay?" Blair asked once we were alone again.

No. I wasn't okay. I had not been okay since I heard the sea elves were back. Then, Lugh had died. Blair could have died too, and now the goddess insisted I was supposed to be crown prince.

No, I wasn't okay. I wouldn't be for a long time.

But I didn't tell her that. "I'll be fine," I lied.

I kicked my horse's flanks and went back to the front of the party, where I hastened our pace so we could get to the coast as soon as possible.

As soon as Red left my side, he sped up the group's pace, and our stop for the night was short, shorter than it should have been. He wanted to arrive at the coast soon, and I couldn't blame him. Even though the sea elves seemed under control right now, as per the report he had heard from his soldier, I understood his need to be there and do something.

We arrived at camp and a horde of soldiers greeted us. Whispers that the rebel prince was here to avenge his brother and save us all spread through the camp. If Red heard the whispers, he pretended he didn't.

Red went directly to the biggest tent in the camp's center. His sleeping tent was right behind it, and mine was right beside his. I ducked under the flap of my tent and stepped in. Sage stayed at the entrance, and I dropped my satchel on the mattress nestled atop red and orange rugs covering the ground. There was a small table with a bowl and a jar on the side. I washed myself, wishing I had time to visit the small pond behind the camp, but I knew Red was at full steam, and if I didn't edge myself into his plans now, I would be left out entirely.

That wasn't me.

Red gathered the generals, captains, and spies in the main tent. He hadn't invited me, but I didn't care. He wouldn't yell at me in front of so many fae.

Regardless, I walked into the main tent as if I belonged there.

As I expected, Red sat behind the long mahogany table, looking at the maps spread out over the table. Lennox was right beside him. General Barric, Captain Runt, Captain Omri, and four other soldiers stood across the table from him, listening to their prince and scouring the maps.

Red's eyes met mine. His lips thinned and his jaw popped. I knew that face. He was mad at me, but as I expected, he didn't say anything. I approached the table and glanced at the map. There were dark blue stones spread over the beach—the sea elves. They had taken a much larger part of the beach than I first thought.

A good way from them was a line of red stones: our soldiers, the ones making sure the sea elves stayed back. And even farther from the line was a bunch of orange stones: this camp.

Afal walked into the tent a few minutes after me.

Red straightened. "Anything different?"

Afal nodded. "The sea elves moved some of their tents

closer to our barrier, my prince. And they seem to be gearing up."

"They are ready to attack," Lennox said.

"I think so," Afal agreed.

Red crossed his arms. "Then we should be ready too. General Barric, tell—"

"Wait." I couldn't help myself. The word flew out of my mouth. Red glared at me as I approached the table and took a good look at the map. I pointed to a few marks on the maps. "Aren't these villages?"

General Barric nodded. "Yes, my lady."

"They are too close," I said. I looked at Red. "If the sea elves advance, there's a chance the villages will be destroyed. The sea elves will target them to hurt us. We should evacuate them first."

"She has a point," Lennox muttered.

"I can't divide the soldiers between evacuating the villages and facing our enemy," Red said, his hazel eyes hard on mine. "To kill them, I'll need every soldier we have."

I squared my shoulders. "I'll do it." Red narrowed his eyes at me. "Sage will go with me."

"That's not enough," Red bristled, his voice tight.

"Then give me a handful of soldiers to help," I suggested. "I know you need them all, but our fae need us too. If I can evacuate them while you get ready for the upcoming battle, then that's one less thing for you to worry about."

"She's right," Lennox said.

"I agree, my prince," General Barric spoke up. "If Lady Blair helps the fae, then we can focus on the fight, and if the fight spills to the villages, we'll have a clear conscience that our fae will survive."

Red stared at me, his eyes still narrowed, his jaw still tight. He was clearly displeased, and for a moment, I didn't know if it was because of my presence here, because he couldn't stand the sight of me, or because I had spoken out of turn. But he had to understand. I wasn't interfering to offend or undermine him. I was doing this for the fae of the Autumn Court. I felt a little lost in my role now that I wasn't queen-to-be anymore, but it didn't matter. I genuinely cared about the Autumn fae, always had, and just because I wouldn't be queen anymore, it didn't mean I stopped caring. Even if I turned out to be one more fae in the kingdom, I would do anything I could to help them. That was my calling.

Red nodded. "Take five soldiers and go."

9

RED

I SAID I would give Blair about five soldiers, but my conscience didn't let me. Instead, I chose fifteen fae I knew by reputation as the most fearless and competent fighters we had.

If General Barric noticed, he didn't say anything.

While Blair went to check something in her tent, I gathered the soldiers and made sure her horse was rested, well fed, and watered. I waited for her with the soldiers at the edge of camp, where a path led to the closest village.

I watched as she walked toward us, weaving among the tents, the soldiers in her way bowing slightly at her, and Sage right behind her, like a stone wall, daring anyone to get close to her. Good.

But despite looking badass in her leather armor, her hair shining under the chilly sunlight, and her eyes even brighter and more determined, Blair acknowledged every one of the soldiers. Some she even called by their names.

I frowned. She probably knew these soldiers better than I did. After all, she had accepted her role and her education, and worked hard at it for many years while I put my tail between my legs and fled the capital as fast as I could.

Blair saw me beside her horse and her brows curled for a moment. If I hadn't been watching so intently, I would have missed it. Her expression smoothed again as she halted in front of me.

"Thank you for selecting the soldiers." She took the reins from me and looked around. "And for giving me more soldiers than you said you would."

"Just ..." I pressed my lips tight, holding the words in. How could I tell her I was proud of her, of her ideals, of her action? How could I tell her I thought she would have made a great queen? How could I tell her I needed her to be careful without showing her my feelings? It was impossible. "Good luck," was all I said.

Blair stared at me for a second, her eyes not betraying any feelings, if she had any left for me. Perhaps I had deluded myself thinking that maybe, just maybe, she had suffered as I had when I left. Perhaps she hadn't even cried, even missed me. The moment I stepped out of her life, out of all of their lives, she simply turned around and fell directly into Lugh's arms.

My stomach clenched and I shook my head once, wishing those thoughts away.

"I will be," she finally said. With impeccable grace, she

swooped up on her horse. She looked at the soldiers. "Everyone ready?"

"Yes, my lady," they all answered.

Blair pulled on the reins and guided her horse toward the path—not once did she look back at me or the camp. Sage and the soldiers followed her.

Worry and longing warred inside me as I watched their procession go, until it disappeared in the distance.

"She'll be fine," Lennox said from behind me.

I steeled myself and turned around. "Who says I'm worried?"

Lennox gave me an are-you-kidding look. "Since when do you lie to me?"

I let out a long sigh. "Sorry. Habit." I glanced back to the path, as if Blair would have come back and I could get one last glance of her. "I didn't expect to have her so close to me all the time." I didn't expect to still have such strong feelings for her. It had been many years since I last held her hand, since I last kissed her. How could I still feel this way? "It's throwing me off my game."

"I know," Lennox said. "Best thing is to find something to do."

I nodded. "Agreed. That's why I'm going to the coast." To show him I was serious, I started walking back to the main tent at the camp's center, where I would tell General Barric about my little excursion.

Lennox fell into step with me. "To check on the sea elves. To see if they have advanced."

"Yes." I knew he would get my plan. "Afal said they are

gathering and arming themselves. I need to see that with my own eyes. Maybe seeing the enemy's faces will spur some idea, and I'll have a brilliant plan about how to blow them off the face of Wyth, so they never come back to haunt the Autumn Court."

Lennox pulled back the tent's flap so I could go under. "That would be a miracle."

THE LINE of Autumn soldiers forming a physical barrier between the sea elves and us wasn't as long as I would like, but we couldn't stretch too thin right now. I stood among them, glancing at the beach several hundred yards from us, where dozens if not hundreds of blue and gray tents had been erected.

The sea elves had gathered near their biggest tent, and all of them had weapons strapped to their armor, and shields nearby. If they weren't going to attack now, they would attack soon.

Still, something didn't feel right. They could easily overcome our barrier of soldiers and overrun our camp—something I planned on correcting as soon as I made my way back there—but they didn't seem in any rush.

"They are up to something," Lennox said from my side.

"Agreed," I muttered. From a distance, the sea elves weren't oblivious. They could see us. They knew we were watching, waiting. But for now, they entertained us with their defiant grins. "I need to find out what."

10

BLAIR

I T DIDN'T TAKE LONG for us to arrive at the first village, Deilen. As soon as we entered the village, some fae recognized me and swarmed around us. At first, Sage and the soldiers yelled at them to stay back.

"No," I said, my word firm. I dismounted and went to greet the fae.

"Lady Blair," an old female fae said, reaching for my hands. "I'm so sorry for your loss." A fat tear rolled down her wrinkled face. "We all loved Crown Prince Lugh."

"We can't believe he is gone," a young male fae said, his eyes equally misted.

Many hands touched my shoulders, my hair, as if I was made of gold and they could steal a little piece by brushing their fingers on it. Many sad and comforting words surrounded me, until I heard something that turned my stomach.

"Now we are left with the rebel prince," an older male fae spat.

"Last I heard, he was in the Winter Court, probably getting drunk and entertaining some sprites," another one said, his words just as upset.

My brows curled down. Yes, Red had abandoned us for a long time—though for most of that time, he had been close by, on the Autumn Court's borders, just out of reach, buried deep inside a soldiers' outpost, pretending he was one of them. But he was here now and he would become the crown prince, and later king of the Autumn Court. I couldn't let our people—his people—think so ill of him.

In the center of the village was a round fountain, with a statue of a small fae child holding up a crescent moon. A trickle of water came out from the moon's edge, falling down at the fountain's lowest level. I pushed through the fae and stepped over the fountain's ledge.

"My dear fae," I called out. Everyone quieted down and looked at me. More fae appeared from within their houses. Some got closer, some stayed by their doors. As long as they all heard me and spread the news, I didn't care where they were. "Our entire kingdom mourns the loss of our beloved Crown Prince Lugh. We'll forever remember him and honor him, and we'll start by doing what he would want us to: accepting the new crown prince with open hearts." Murmurs started and I continued, "Prince Redlen is here, at this moment, ready to protect us from their attacks. He came as soon as he heard about the sea elves, even before Prince

Lugh had fallen. He came because he loves the Autumn Court, because he believes in us, because he wanted to be beside his brother while they drove the enemy back." My words broke, and I inhaled deeply, forcing myself to stay steady. "Prince Lugh isn't among us anymore, but Prince Redlen is, and he'll do anything to protect us, to protect you."

Again, voices peppered the crowd. A few people said "shush" and silence fell around us once again.

"And, because this village is too close to the coast, the first thing Prince Redlen wanted us to do is to evacuate." I braced myself for the whiplash. There were no murmurs this time, but plain shouts and disagreement.

"Leave? We can't leave."

"Where will we go?"

"What about my shop?"

"I have work to do."

"If I leave, who will take care of my cattle?"

"I can't abandon my house."

"Listen!" I called out again. "Please, listen," I tried again. The soldiers took a step closer, advancing on the circle of fae, and they all quieted down again. "I know this is scary, and sudden, but it's for your safety. The sea elves have already tricked us once, we don't want them to do that again by attacking us where it hurts the most—our own fae. Houses and businesses are important and valuable, but they can be replaced. You can't be replaced. So, please, listen to me. Pack your things and let's leave within the hour. We'll march toward Masarn, where you will be lodged in a shelter and provided for while this situation lasts." I paused. "I promise we'll do everything in our power to help you with your houses and businesses after the sea elves are gone." The murmurs started again. "Hopefully, this is a preventive measure, and they won't come this way."

It took me another short speech to see the fae finally moving. They went back into their houses to pack, though a few of them didn't move. They proclaimed they wouldn't leave, no matter what.

My patience was thin as I talked to them, trying to convince them otherwise.

The soldiers and I helped the fae pack, prepared the horses, fill out wagons with their clothes, food, and children, and head toward the road leading to the capital in the center of the kingdom. But they weren't going fast enough. An hour passed, and we had not evacuated a fourth of the village. And I still had a handful of other villages to stop by before nightfall. If things continued this way, it would take me at least three days to visit all of the villages and convince the fae to leave.

After another hour of mulling over, I turned to a handful of soldiers who were close by. "Things are in motion here. We need to get to the other villages. Five of you stay here and make sure everyone evacuates and heads to the capital. The rest of us will go to the next village. When you're done here, meet us there."

"Yes, my lady," a soldier replied.

The moment we left the village behind and hit the road to the next one, Sage pulled his horse closer to mine. "Do you think it's wise to separate like that, my lady?"

"No, but we have to speed things up," I said. Actually, my plan was to spread thin. I would arrive at the next village, talk to the fae, but I wouldn't help. Instead, I would leave another five soldiers to help them while the remaining five soldiers, Sage and I went on to the next village. This way, we could set more things in motion, and have more fae safe faster. I knew this was preventive work. Hopefully, evacuating was a precaution, but I couldn't help feeling like it should be done. "We have to."

Sage didn't argue with me. He rarely did.

The next village received us a little better than the last one, and most fae were moving and packing before I had finished my speech. I left the five soldiers who were accompanying me there, and went on to the next village.

Niwl was the smallest of the villages along the coast-line, but also the closest to the beach. Like the other two villages, most fae recognized me the instant I trotted into the village, and they welcomed me with open arms. Since here there were no fountains I could use as a dais, I stayed on my horse.

"Dear Niwl fae, as you know, the sea elves have come to our shores again," I started, my voice rasping against my throat. I had been talking more and louder than usual since morning. "We need to prepare and—"

A shriek cut through the air and I swallowed me words. The fae stilled and Sage pulled out his sword. The soldiers closed in around me.

In matter of seconds, yells started and footsteps echoed through the village.

Sea elves emerged from between the houses and buildings, and surrounded us.

Their weapons trained on me.

One of the sea elves stepped closer, and I recognized him. Ta'hun. The sea elf who had killed Lugh.

He bared his sharp teeth in a grin. "We meet again, princess."

I GOT BACK into the camp, ready to call on the generals and captains and lay out a complex plan to push the sea elves back where they came from—and kill as many of them as we could in the process. But as soon as I entered the main tent and opened my mouth, a soldier rushed in, out of breath.

"Your Highness," he rasped. "Sea elves were waiting. They ambushed Lady Blair."

"What?" I froze, every muscle in my body locked up. "What did you say?"

"Lady Blair had just arrived in Niwl when the sea elves surrounded her." He took a deep breath before continuing, "I was sent back to warn you and ask for help."

He didn't have to say it twice. Knowing my feelings, Lennox ran out of the tent faster than me and started calling soldiers by name—all of them shapeshifters.

I didn't wait for them to gather. I simply shifted into my

fox and raced out of the camp and toward Niwl as fast as I could. I knew Lennox and the others were following me, just as fast, but there was only one thing on my mind right now.

Please, Blair, be safe.

It didn't take long for me to reach Niwl, though at the same time, it seemed like an eternity had passed and anything could have happened. From the road, I could see the dark smoke rising into the sky—the village was on fire. I sped up, my legs hurting from the effort.

To my surprise, Blair and Sage were outside the village, on the road, fighting the sea elves with the soldiers and some villagers. More fae ran from the village and into the forest beyond it, trying to escape from the enemy.

Instant relief filled my chest, along with determination. She was fine, but now it was time to show these rusting sea elves what Autumn fae were made of.

As I approached, Blair brought her hands up and a gust of chilly wind blasted over the sea elves advancing on them. Many red and orange leaves swirling in the wind, cutting the sea elves on the face and arms and hands like paper.

I shifted back into my fae form the moment I reached Blair's side. She didn't acknowledge me or stop fighting. I, though, took a second as I recognized the bodies of two of our soldiers, three villagers, and a handful of sea elves at our feet.

Rust.

Falling into battle mode instantly, I called more wind.

A strong squall swirled around the sea elves, pushing them back.

I drew my sword up and yelled, "For the Autumn Court!"

The soldiers and I advanced, engaging the sea elves before they recovered from the wind and leaves. Some tried to run—were they fleeing?—but I didn't let them. I lifted my hands and brown roots shot out from the ground, wrapping around the ankles and legs of the sea elves. Around me, my soldiers gifted with magic did the same.

Our blades cut through the enemy and killed them.

When there was only a dozen or so left, a sea elf yelled and ran toward Blair. I swung my sword across the chest of the sea elf in front of me, then ran after him.

Fighting another sea elf, Blair had her back to the incoming sea elf.

"Blair!" I called.

But it cost her. She lost focus on her first opponent, and now had a second one to worry about. Sage was preoccupied with two enemies, who kept trying to reach Blair.

They knew who she was.

They probably knew who I was too.

"Hey!" I called once I was within range. The second opponent turned to me. He was taller than me, with longer limbs, longer ears, and incredibly sharp teeth. "Fight me."

"Of course, my prince," he said in a thick accent and a sly grin.

"That's Ta'hun," Blair said, while ducking from a strike. "He's the one who killed Lugh."

I inhaled deeply. Bright red clouded my vision.

"Nice to meet you, little prince." Ta'hun bowed slightly. Oh, he was done for.

I charged.

But the rusting sea elf was ready for it. He sidestepped and pulled his own soldier in my way. I careened into the other sea elf, losing my balance for a moment. The sea elf punched my stomach, pushing the air out of my lungs. Doubling over, I gasped. I blinked, trying to recover. The sea elf came at me, but then Lennox was by my side in his fox form. With his fangs bared, Lennox jumped on the side of the sea elf and bit his flesh. The sea elf howled.

I turned to Ta'hun, who was already in motion. He had a spear in his hand and he took aim: Blair.

"No," I whispered.

My legs pushed and I ran the short distance as fast as I could. He threw the spear at Blair, who was busy fighting another sea elf. She didn't see the spear that would strike her chest.

That would kill her.

Knowing I wouldn't make it in time, I waved my hand and sent a blast of wind to the spear. It moved to the side, missed Blair by an inch, and ended up buried in the shoulder of the sea elf she had been fighting.

Wide-eyed, Blair turned. "What the ...?"

Ta'hun reached her and brought his axe down on her. Blair raised her sword, but Ta'hun kicked her in the chest and struck the hilt of his axe at her head.

Blair went down.

I raced toward Ta'hun. He smiled at me, taunting me, and then he ran. All of the sea elves did. They turned and ran, going for the beach again.

What was that about?

I didn't waste time thinking about why they up and left—dwindling numbers maybe? Instead, I knelt beside Blair.

"Blair," I called as I touched her neck and checked her pulse. It was strong. I exhaled in relief, realizing she had fainted. Gently, I picked her up in my arms and stood. I faced my soldiers, who were as baffled as me. "Clean up this mess, check to see if anyone is infected, help the villagers finish evacuating. Then come back to the camp."

"Yes, my prince," General Barric said.

Sage was the only one who followed Blair and me back to the camp.

BEFORE I FULLY WOKE UP, I registered the dull pain on the back of my head. By the fallen leaves, that hurt. What a miserable—

I opened my eyes, remembering everything that had happened. The village, the sea elves, the fire, the screams, Red arriving and helping, the rusting sea elf knocking me out.

Then darkness.

The second thing I registered was that I wasn't alone on the mattress in my tent. Red sat a few inches from my waist, at the edge of the mattress, his eyes closed and his hand on top of mine.

I didn't know if he was sleeping or resting his eyes, but I took advantage of this moment to take a good look at him. Besides the sweat and the splat of blood on his neck and the sleeves of his tunic, he still took my breath away. He had always been handsome, but somehow he was much more gorgeous now. The sharp angles of his face were sharper, his eyebrows full, his lips fuller, his lashes even longer, and the stubble over his jaw and chin gave him an air of being older, wiser, and rougher.

My fingers itched to reach up and run over his face, down his powerful shoulders, press against his chest—

His eyes snapped open. Red caught me staring at him.

"You're awake." He shifted on the mattress, straightening his back and pulling his hand from mine. "How are you feeling? How's your head?"

"Never mind my head, what happened to the village?" I sat up and a rush of dizziness assaulted me. I gritted my teeth and pushed it away. "Were we able to evacuate all the fae?"

One corner of Red's lip curled up. "You got hurt, and your first question is about others. No wonder everyone was so eager to have you as queen."

I frowned. "You didn't answer me."

"We lost three fae, along with a handful of soldiers," he told me, his voice hard again. "But we killed more of them. There were plenty of sea elf bodies for us to burn."

I pressed a hand to my chest. "Thank the red leaves." Red grew serious. His jaw ticked as it usually did when he was keeping something in. I almost rolled my eyes at him. "What is it?"

Exhaling, he ran a hand through his messy hair. "I can't believe you ditched most of the soldiers and went ahead with Sage."

"Sage and I are capable and—"

Red shot to his feet. "I know you can fight, and I know Sage is one of the best soldiers in the entire kingdom—that's the reason he was assigned to you, after all—but still, Blair, you can't put yourself in this position."

"Why not? I'm not queen-to-be anymore. And if I have to choose between my life and the fae, it'll always be the fae."

Red clenched his fists and he turned his back to me, muttering under his breath. A few seconds passed before he finally turned to me again. "You should rest—"

"The rake I will." I put my feet down and started to get up. "There's lot to do and—" I shut up as my head swam and black spots filled my vision.

"Blair," Red hissed. In a flash, he was in front of me, holding my hands in his. "You need to rest. Please."

"I will rest when I'm dead." My eyes widened and I took a step back, pulling my hands from his and almost falling on the mattress again. "Did you have a healer check me? I'm not sick, am I? Stay away until we find out."

He stared at me for a moment before finally speaking. "If you were sick, I wouldn't care."

What did he mean he wouldn't care? If I was sick, he had to either isolate me before I infected him or anyone else. Or he had to kill me. Really, killing me would be more merciful.

He reached forward and held my hands again. I jerked against him. "Red, let go!"

"I won't," he said, his eyes locked on mine. I lost the fight against that intense gaze and stilled. My breathing grew shallow. "But yes, I had a healer check you, and I sent a healer to the fae who evacuated from the villages to check them before they proceeded to the capital."

I relaxed, but just a little. Sometimes, the sea plague started slowly. We still hadn't found a cure for it. We had medicine that slowed its spread and relieved the pain a little bit, but we couldn't stop it. Eventually, it killed everyone who contracted it.

"Then, if I'm fine, we need to resume work," I said, though deep down, I was quite enjoying this moment and his closeness. "We have much to do."

Again, a corner of his lips tugged up. "You're impossible."

That was amusing? Suddenly irritated, I jerked against him. I was able to free one hand and used it to push him back. "Look who is talking! You're the rebel."

"Don't call me that," he hissed between gritted teeth.

I stepped closer, lifting my chin in defiance. "Why not? Isn't it true?"

His eyes searched mine for a moment, though I had no idea what he was looking for. "It is. Let me show you how much of a rebel I can be."

Before I blinked, Red's hand clasped the nape of my neck and he pulled me to him. My body crushed against him and his mouth descended on mine.

It took me a second to register what was happening, but once I did, I felt like I had no will to fight this. Not when his hard body was pressed against mine, when his other hand snaked around my waist and splayed on the small of my back, pulling me even closer, when his soft lips moved against mine with such thirst.

I was a goner.

I held on to his broad shoulders and parted my lips, welcoming him. His tongue invaded my mouth and my knees buckled. By the chilly wind, this felt so familiar and yet so different, so intense ...

We had been so young when we first fell in love, so stupid. Back then, his kisses had been good, but not this good. Now, he could make me moan and weep with how gloriously his lips and his tongue played with mine.

Suddenly, it was all gone.

Red jumped several feet back. He stared at me with wide eyes. "That ..." He shook his head and averted his eyes. "That shouldn't have happened. I'm sorry."

Without looking at me, Red marched out of my tent.

I was left alone with my desire and my shame.

13

RED

I RAN from Blair's tent as if it was on fire. Because it was. Maybe not literally, but it was. The heat she brought up inside my core was too much to handle.

Lennox fell into step with me. "How is she?"

"Impossible," I snapped. Suddenly, I halted and told him, "Gather some of our best scouts. I want to patrol the forest to make sure no more sea elves are hiding and waiting to ambush us."

"Yes." He turned to leave, but when I continued toward my tent, he stopped. "Aren't you coming?"

"In a moment," was all I said.

Without giving Lennox another thought, I entered my tent and started pacing, my mind reeling, my feelings too raw to handle.

Why, oh, why did I feel like I had no control around Blair? Why did I say things I shouldn't? Why did I touch her at any opportunity? Why had I kissed her?

I halted in the middle of my tent and ran a hand down my face. Rust, after so long, she still got under my skin like nothing else, like no one else. She had meant the world to me. She had been my everything.

Apparently, she still was.

And now that we were older, there was more—a raw need, a deep desire, a want that hurt.

Rust, I couldn't join the scouts and go sea elf hunting like this.

Knowing no one would bother me right now, I sat in the armchair and pulled the waist of my pants down a little. I snaked my hand inside my underpants and wrapped my fingers along my cock. Just thinking of Blair, of that kiss, of her mouth on mine, made me hard and ready. I had lost count of how many times I had done this the past few years. I thought about Blair, got hot and bothered, and had to relieve myself to get her out of my system. Now with her right here, so close, and after that kiss ... I groaned and started moving my hand. Up and down, hard and fast, while I imagined not only kissing her, but also stripping her of clothes, laying her on my bed, covering her body with mine. Rust, that drove me crazy. I closed my eyes and threw my head back as the desire in my body built up, as my cock became harder and harder. Would she moan in my ear if I took her? Would she graze her long nails on my back and shoulders? Oh, rust.

I jerked as I came, harder and stronger than I had in a long time. And it was because of that rusting kiss.

The tremors in my body lessened and I stayed in the

chair for a while longer, swimming in that haze, feeling relaxed and spent, but also relieved.

Although, I knew my hand would never make up for the real thing.

LENNOX, the scouts, and I spent the entire night running through the orange and red forest, searching for those rusting sea elves, but we found none. We also didn't find any trails that indicated more had come farther into the kingdom.

When the sun started rising on the horizon, sending the chill of the night away, and tinting everything with golden light, Lennox and I stopped at the barrier set up along the coast.

"Have they moved?" I asked one of the captains stationed there.

"No, my prince," he answered, his tone firm. "They keep displaying their weapons, play-fighting among themselves, grinning at us as if they know something we don't, but they haven't left the beach."

That was strange. Why would our enemies invade our beaches and stay there? So far, they had tricked us at Caer Mor and Niwl. I knew they were setting up another trick, I just didn't know what.

"What about our spy?" I asked. It was hard to have spies among the sea elves since we looked so different, but we had found a soldier who, with a little makeup and a change of clothes, could pass as one of them. We had sent him to the enemy almost a day ago.

"We haven't heard from him yet, my prince," the captain said. "I don't think we will for a while."

Me neither. Besides that, even if he made into their ranks, he wouldn't be able to get close to their leaders to find out what they were up to. Not in a short time, anyway.

I stayed with the barrier soldiers most of the day, observing our enemies. They really didn't do anything other than show off their weapons and armor, and duel like I had been doing in the Winter Court.

In the middle of the afternoon, I returned to our camp. My current plan was to gather the generals and captains and the scouts and draw a plan. Waiting for them to attack wasn't working.

Lennox and I had just entered the main tent when a soldier rushed in.

"My prince, I'm sorry for barging in, but I thought you would like to know," he said, his head low.

I sat down on one of the chairs around the table. "What is it?"

"It's Lady Blair, my prince."

I stilled. "What is it? Is she still ill?"

"No, my prince, quite the contrary." He paused, lifted his eyes to mine, and quickly lowered them again. "Not long after the sun rose this morning, she left with her protector."

I pushed up to my feet. "Where did she go?"

"She went to check on the villagers, make sure everyone had evacuated and that no one was sick."

I cursed under my breath. Of course she wouldn't believe me. Of course she had to check for herself. Of course she had to do the queenly thing. Of course she had to ignore her own health for her people.

"Inform me the moment she returns to camp," I told the soldier, then I waved my hand, dismissing him.

He stepped out of the tent, and Lennox turned to me. "And here I thought you would fox-up and go after her."

"Believe me, I want to." It took every ounce of control I had not to. "I'll give her another hour."

The sunset wasn't too far away and having her roaming the roads at night while our enemy was so close was dangerous. She might not be destined to be queen anymore, but she was a symbol to our kingdom. The fae loved her as much as they had loved Lugh.

I ran a hand over my face. Rust, why did it have to be Lugh? He was doing so well. He would have made a great king, and beside Blair, they would have made the Autumn Court proud and strong.

Why couldn't it have been me instead?

I let out a long sigh. Lennox knew me too well, because he brought a jug of spiced wine and glasses for us, then took a seat across the table from me. I filled my glass to the brim and gulped half of the wine in one go.

Lennox raised an eyebrow at me. "Something is troubling you. Or should I say someone?"

"Don't even start." I groaned. "I wish Blair was one of those court ladies who like dresses, teas, and parties."

"Then you wouldn't like her the way you do."

"That's my point exactly."

Lennox stared at his glass. "I remember the day we left the capital and practically jumped headfirst into the army and never looked back."

Me too. How could I forget? That was the day my parents announced Blair was betrothed to my brother.

I let out a long sigh, and the memories flooded my mind before I could stop them. Blair's father had been a close advisor to my father, one of his closest friends. It was only natural that since her birth, Blair frequented the palace. As a little kid, I thought she was annoying, but that was because she was a female wanting to do everything a male did. Lugh always thought she was amazing, despite the age difference between them.

But as we grew, she transformed from an ugly duck to a dazzling swan, and she still liked sword fighting, shooting arrows, and running, which enticed me. Though, because of her age, she was forced to participate in more teas and other female duties within the court. She didn't exactly hate those. She performed her job well, but the moment she could, she escaped to play with Lugh and me. Maize was younger than us and tried to keep up, but when we could, we left her behind. Before I knew it, I was falling for Blair. Thankfully, Lugh had expressed several times that he liked her as a sister, and as far as I knew, he had eyes on a young female librarian. I was sad for him because, as the crown prince, he would never be allowed to marry her.

But at least he hadn't shown any interest in Blair. Or she in him. Lugh was already being trained as the crown prince and had more duties, classes, and training every month, leaving Blair to play with me alone. It didn't take long to realize Blair seemed to like that.

We got older, and I started my military training, and Blair attended more duties and events with the court ladies. But whenever we could, we met up. We weren't kids anymore, but we spent time together. We sat on the fountain in the middle of the garden, or adventured into the forest, found a tall tree and raced to the top, or went out hunting critters with our bows.

One evening, after we spent the entire day running from our duties and hunting in the forest, Blair and I stopped by the lake behind the palace. Wearing only her chemise, Blair was the first in the water. When she dove and emerged from the water in the center of the lake, her hair almost black and her chemise transparent at her shoulders, and smiled at me, I knew my heart was lost forever.

I made my way to her, giving her every opportunity to step back or stop me, but she didn't. I kissed her and she kissed me back. In that moment, I knew I loved her, had loved her for a long time, and my heart would forever be hers.

A couple of weeks later, our parents announced Blair had been chosen as Lugh's betrothed, and my heart was ripped from my chest. Lugh assured me he'd had no idea, and as soon as he heard about it, he tried undoing it, but the elders disagreed with him. I argued with my father and my mother, without telling them the truth, but they dismissed it as if I was a spoiled child.

When I realized that nothing would change their mind, that the fae I loved would marry my brother, bear him children, and spend the rest of her life with him, I left.

I left because I couldn't watch it.

Lennox, being my best friend besides Blair, left with me. I always assumed that had been an excuse. Lennox had come from a simple family, and he had promised his parents to find a better life. He wanted to be a famous soldier, and following a rebel prince on his quest to hide in the training fields was the quickest way to do that. Well, he achieved that. Because he was my right and left arms, Lennox's name was known throughout Wyth.

And my nickname too.

"That was a long time ago," I whispered.

"And yet, your feelings for her are still the same."

"Are you still jealous of her?" I teased. Back in the day, he had always complained I preferred Blair's company to his. Well, I could kiss her, couldn't I? I didn't want to do that with him.

"Now it's not jealousy—it's worry."

I scoffed. "Don't worry. Nothing will happen."

He leaned forward, crossing his arms over the table. "It won't. Because now she's practically a widow, and you're the one who will inherit the kingdom. Depending on your choice, her path doesn't need to change."

I frowned. As if I hadn't thought of that already. But it didn't feel right. She had been promised to Lugh. What if in the time I was away, they had fallen in love? What if they had even mated, and I didn't know? A lot could have happened in the time I avoided them all.

Besides, Blair was supposed to be mourning right now. It was disrespectful to think of her that way when my brother had just died.

"I don't want to think about that," I muttered before raising my glass to my lips and draining the rest of my drink.

"I know you don't, but at some point, you'll have to. After we kill all of the sea elves and our kingdom is safe again, you'll have to face the inevitable: You'll become crown prince and you'll have to figure out what to do with her. As your best friend and advisor, I'm here to remind you of that, to make sure you really think this through and don't make a rash decision."

"Like what?"

He shrugged. "I don't know. Sending her to a nunnery so the temptation of sleeping with your brother's fiancée is far away?"

I wrinkled my nose. Only Lennox could make things sound even worse than they were. "Just ... shut up."

I reached for the jug and poured more wine into my glass. But before I could raise my glass, Afal stepped into the tent. "Lady Blair is back, my prince."

My muscles tensed and I almost jumped from my chair. I resisted that impulse. "Thank you."

Afal bowed his head and stepped out.

Lennox reached for my glass. "Here. I'll help you." He drank it all in one gulp. "Now go see if your love is well."

I shot him a glare. "Anyone else talking to me like that would have lost his head."

With a smug grin, Lennox leaned back in his chair and brought his feet up on the table. "I'm glad I'm not anyone else."

Shaking my head, I walked out of the tent. I didn't even know what I would say to Blair, other than order her to stay back, to rest, to go back to the capital. Having her here was too distracting. I couldn't come up with a good plan because I was busy either being worried about her or being attracted to her.

She would yell, she would argue, but I was done. I would even use my next-crown-prince's-order excuse if I had to. And she would have to listen.

I paused at the entrance to her tent and let out a long sigh.

I *hoped* she would listen to me.

14

BLAIR

It had been a long day.

Once I learned Red had spent the night out and still hadn't come back when the sun rose, I got up and did something. Staying in bed and resting wasn't my style, even if I was still a little hurt and sore from the last fight. No, I had to do something, to feel useful.

So, I went to the villages with Sage, making sure all the fae had left, and that the ones who had had contact with the sea elves had been checked or were in observation for the sea plague. The last thing we needed was an outbreak of the illness right now.

Sage had grilled me about leaving without at least double the soldiers from the other day, but I had heard what Red had been doing all night: checking the forest to make sure no other sea elf was hiding and waiting to ambush us. Besides, the sea elves had attacked us that day. They wouldn't use the same tactic so soon.

It didn't take long for me to feel even sorer and more tired, but it didn't matter. I pushed through because the fae needed me. They had been forced from their homes and were headed to shelters in the capital for who knew how long. Their entire lives had turned upside down, and their businesses would probably suffer when they came back. Checking on them, making sure they were fine and healthy, and they had everything they needed to the trip to the capital was the least I could do.

Midday, Sage and I rested a little beside a stream. After I took a short nap, Sage stood watch while I washed in the cold water. Finally, when the sun started descending, Sage bugged me to return to the camp. "It'll be dark when we arrive. I don't want you to stay out after that."

I knew he wouldn't let it go, so I relented.

The moment we arrived at the camp, I saw soldiers eyeing us and a couple even ran to the main tent, probably to warn Red that I was back. I didn't pay much attention to them since they were following orders. I handed my horse to one of them and went to my tent.

Even though I had washed at the stream, I was in desperate need for clean clothes. I took off my boots, untied my pants, pulled them off, undid the clasps of my vest and tunic, and my tunic slipped off my shoulders—then someone walked in my tent.

Red's eyes went wide as I slapped my hands over myself, holding the tunic before it fell and exposed my torso. But the vest hit the floor. Red's eyes only grew wider as they traveled down to my bare legs—my tunic's hem barely hit my thighs.

"I-I'm sorry," he whispered, turning around and reaching for the tent's opening.

"No, wait," I blurted. He stopped, but didn't look at me. I reached for a silk robe, let the tunic fall all the way, and put the robe on. I made sure I tied it tightly around my waist before saying, "It's okay now."

Red turned again, this time his eyes fixed on my face, as if he was trying hard not to look at my body. Something like disappointment bloomed in my chest.

"Hm, I came to check on you," he said. Then he frowned. "Aren't you still weak and hurt? Why the rake were you out all day? And what about warning me, or letting me borrow more soldiers? And where is Sage? He wasn't outside your tent."

"I told him to go rest. I didn't think I needed him for a few hours in a camp full of highly trained soldiers." I lifted my chin. "I don't need babysitters all the time, Red."

"Are you sure? Think about what happened not even two days ago!"

"The sea elves had planned on taking the villages long before I planned on evacuating them. Me being there was a coincidence. Besides, I know you spent last night searching for them from the coast to the forest beyond the villages. If you had found anything, I would have heard. I knew it was safe."

Red pressed his lips tight, clearly wanting to argue. "Is

there anything I can say to convince you to go back to the capital?"

I shook my head. "You might not like it, but I'm not a cowering court lady. I prefer being here, getting my hands dirty, and actually helping."

"I know," he muttered.

"Is that so horrible?"

Letting out a long breath, Red ran a hand through his hair. "Quite the opposite. You're amazing." My breath caught. Realizing what he had said, Red shifted his weight from foot to foot. "I mean ..."

I knew what he meant. At least, I hoped I did.

Emboldened by the way he had looked at me, by his words, I took two steps toward him, leaving a short space between us. If I extended my arm, I could rest my hand on his chest.

I fixed my eyes on his. "Just ... stay where you are."

I untied my robe and let it fall to my feet. Red's eyes bugged, but I didn't give him a chance to react. Instead, I wrapped my arms around his neck and pulled him to me. I pressed my mouth to his.

Red moved his lips with mine for before pulling back. "No, no. This isn't right."

I held on to his shoulders. "Why not?"

"You ... you're promised to my brother."

I shook my head. "He isn't here anymore. Besides, I never loved him." I tugged his shoulders again. When he didn't resist, I glued my body to his and kissed him again.

This time, Red's hands wrapped around my waist in a

flash, his rough palms grazing against my skin, sending shivers down my spine.

I knew it. I knew he wanted me as much as I wanted him.

His lips moved against mine, his tongue assaulting my mouth, his scent invading my nostrils and intoxicating my mind. Kissing Red was the right thing, the perfect thing. It felt like he was made for me.

Slowly, I slid my hands down his chest to his waist. I found the buttons of his leather pants. Then, I broke the kiss and knelt in front of him, while undoing the buttons and pushing his pants down.

"Blair," he hissed.

But he didn't stop me. Good.

His cock was hard and big, bigger than I expected, but that didn't stop me. I wrapped my hand around it, and licked the tip. Red jerked and hissed. I licked his length once more before taking it all inside my mouth.

"Rust." Red knotted his fingers on my hair.

I started moving, taking him in and out of my mouth, as far as I could, with my hand tight around the shaft, putting more pressure on his cock.

"Oh, rust," he muttered again. I spied on him. Red had his eyes closed, his face tilted upward, his mouth hanging open, and his hands in my hair. It was a sight to behold. The way he seemed to be undone emboldened me. I liked knowing I could do this to him.

I sped up, moving my mouth along his cock faster, harder.

Then, he clasped his hands around my shoulders and pushed me back. I glanced up and found him staring at me. "That was amazing, but I don't want to finish that way." He slid his hands down my elbow and helped me up.

I barely stood up before he was on me, his mouth on mine, his body pressed against mine. While drinking from each other, I helped Red take off his vest and his tunic. I ran my hands around his shoulders, his chest, his back, trying to feel every inch of him, every chisel of every muscle and commit it to memory. By the chilly wind, this fae had been carved out of stone.

Red broke the kiss, but stayed close, his forehead resting on mine. "Now, it's my turn."

I TRIED TO FIGHT IT. All day and all night, I tried to fight it.

After that kiss last night, every cell and pore in my body had felt alive. Bothered. Hot. In disarray.

It didn't matter how hard I fought. I ended up losing. In this moment, what really mattered was that I wanted Blair like I had never wanted anything, anyone, in my entire life.

When it came to her, I was weak after all.

Blair let out a little gasp before I closed my mouth around hers again. I slid my hands down, down, down to her thighs, and she let me lift up her legs. She wound them around my waist, and when I pressed my body to hers, putting my hard-on right on the perfect spot, she gasped again.

I pushed my hips against hers again, teasing her. Blair arched her back in response, throwing her head back. I couldn't resist that long, smooth neck and slid my lips from her mouth to her neck. I licked and nipped her soft skin, enjoying how she squirmed under my touch, how her breathing grew shallow and erratic and how warm her skin was.

I straightened up and rested her back on one of the thick column holding the tent up, just enough so I could take off my leather vest and pull my tunic over my head. All the while, Blair's eyes were fixed on mine, a shine in them I had never seen before. A deep, warm gaze that made me even harder for her.

Then I stayed there, while her legs were around my waist, our hips naked and touching, and her back leaned against the door, admiring the beautiful fae in front of me.

Rust, this fae.

Her breasts were perfect and perky, and her thin waist and flat stomach completed the package.

"You're so beautiful," I uttered.

She gave me a crooked smile. "And you too hot." She reached over and hooked her hand on my neck. "Now, come back here." She tugged and I let her pull me to her.

I crashed my mouth to hers, kissing her even harder and deeper than before. Blair moved her hips, and I groaned as the friction on my cock increased. I slipped my hands up her waist and cupped her breasts. Damn, they were made for my hands. I pinched the nipples and she let out a little cry against my mouth.

Rust.

"Come here." I wound my arms around her back and kept her up, her legs around my waist, as I pushed away from the column. Holding her tight, I walked to the mattress, and deposited her over the soft covers. Then, I scooted her to the edge and knelt between her parted legs.

Blair sucked in a sharp breath.

I leaned into her legs—she bit her lower lip and I almost crawled over her to capture that lip myself, but I wanted to pleasure her first—and kissed the inside of her thighs. Blair hissed and tensed and hissed some more, while I tortured her, inching up to her center agonizingly slow. Finally, I licked her clit. Moaning, Blair arched her back. She reached down and wound her fingers into my hair. Enjoying how she was unraveling with each of my touches, I worked her. I slipped a finger inside her, then a second one, and I chuckled when she cursed and moaned. I pumped my fingers fast, while sucking and licking and kissing and nipping at her sensitive spot.

I felt her body tensing as her climax built.

"Harder," she whispered.

I obliged and thrust my fingers harder, while I sucked on her clit. With a cry, Blair stilled for a second, then broke down in little quivers.

She was still trembling when I crawled over her, planting small kisses all over her body—her hip bone, her navel, her ribs, her breasts. There, I paused. I licked around the under edge of her left breast, while I clasped the other with my hand. Then, I closed my mouth around the nipple and sucked. Arching her back, Blair let out a cry. I sucked, I kissed, I licked, and all the while she squirmed under me, her long nails trailing paths on my back, leaving their mark.

I continued up my path. I kissed her collarbone, the soft spot between her shoulder and neck, her jaw, her chin, and finally her mouth. She smiled, and when I pulled back, she wound her arms around my neck and pulled me to her again. This time I smiled before she kissed me.

While kissing me, she parted her legs. I adjusted myself, and with a groan, I inched inside her. Very, very slow. Blair held her breath until I had buried my cock inside her. Rust, this fae. So tight. So wet. So perfect. I dropped my head to her shoulder, trying to get used to the pressure, to her.

Then two things happened almost at the same time. One, Blair tensed in a way I could only associate with one thing.

"You're a virgin," I whispered, a little shocked. We hadn't gone that far when we were younger, but for some reason, I had assumed that by now, she would have slept with someone else.

"Of course I am. Was."

And two, she gasped, as the force, that invisible line, thick and eternal and unmistakable, formed between us.

"The bond." I looked into her eyes, more shocked now. "The mating bond."

Blair smiled at me, a wicked thing, a beautiful thing. I started pulling back, trying to comprehend this new level of complexity, but Blair hooked her legs around my waist and tugged me back to her. "No, don't." She wrapped her arms around my neck. "Stay with me," she whispered in my ear. She squirmed her hips, increasing the rusting pressure on my cock.

How could I resist this? Resist her?

A possessive feeling gripped my gut. I was Blair's first. I hated to admit that made me proud and a little crazier about her.

She might be a virgin, but she knew exactly what she was doing to me. She lifted her hips, driving my cock even deeper.

"Rust," I hissed.

"Move," she whispered, breathless. "Please, move."

How could I say no to that?

I lifted my torso on my elbows and looked at her, into her beautiful amber eyes, at the lust and desire shining in them and driving me crazy. I pulled all the way back, then slammed into her again. Gasping, Blair cupped my ass and pulled me toward her. I started moving, slow for only two long thrusts, before I couldn't keep this up anymore. I had to have her, and I had to have all of her now.

I thrust into her deep and hard and fast.

"Yes," Blair said, her voice low.

"Rust, I know." I leaned into her and caught her mouth with mine. I plunged my tongue into her mouth, just like me, hard and deep and fast. She buried her nails in my back and the pain mixed with the pleasure.

I was ready to dive into this beautiful fae, I was ready to give in to the pleasure building in my core, to let it all go and swim in pure bliss, when Blair clutched my shoulders, and using a fighting move, turned us around. My back hit the mattress and she straddled me.

"Rusting ..."

She looked down at me, with a naughty smile on his lips. Her long hair fell around her shoulders and down her back, and her lean torso was straight as a board. She pushed down on me, and I groaned with how deep she could take it like this.

She started moving. Slow at first, with long, deliberate strokes. But then she hissed and, looking into my eyes, she sped up—virgin? She was a virgin? That was hard to believe, but oh, it made me feel so proud and possessive right now.

Her breasts bounced with each up and down, up and down. I reached over and clasped her breasts. I pinched her nipples, and moaning, she threw her head back.

I slid my hands down to her waist and I helped her move, pulling her down hard. Harder, deeper. The tension built up, stronger and faster this time.

Blair leaned forward and rested her hands on my shoulders, her hair falling beside us like a curtain. She pressed down with her hands and used that as leverage to move even faster and deeper.

Rust, this fae.

I felt it ... I felt the tension in her building too. I felt her walls tightening. I heard her breath growing erratic and her moans louder. Then, with one last push, she cried out. She fell over, her chest on mine. I clutched her waist and thrust once, twice, three more times. She bit my neck and that did it.

The pleasure in me burst and my body trembled uncontrollably.

When the spasms slowed, I cupped Blair's neck and pulled her face to mine. I captured her mouth with mine, kissing her slow and deep, savoring her sweet taste and the warmth of her body.

Rust, we had barely finished and I wanted more. I wanted much more of her, from her.

She then pulled back and crossed her arms on my chest, resting her chin on her forearm. A small smile adorned her lips. "So you are my mate."

My gut tightened. "I am."

I am, I repeated to myself.

"Are you surprised?" she asked, running her nails over my stomach, and sending shivers up my spine.

"Honestly, no." It was the truth. I always thought that if someone was my mate, it had to be Blair. But then when she was promised to Lugh, I pushed that idea aside.

"Me neither," she whispered.

I frowned. "Blair, about us—"

She stilled. "Don't you dare say this was a mistake."

"No, it wasn't a mistake," I said. Her eyes rounded. I was a little surprised by my own words too. "Anything with you is never a mistake. But there are still too many things that need resolving and—"

"I understand." She started pulling away. I reached for her and held her close to me.

"I don't think you do. Whatever happens, I don't think I can let go of you, not anymore. I'm asking for patience while I navigate this new world. Deal?"

One corner of her lips curled up. "Deal."

I stared at her, once again, struck by how beautiful she was. "By the chilly wind, I can't resist you."

I clasped my hand behind her neck, brought my lips to hers, and turned us around on the mattress, so my body was flush with hers, my cock at the right place.

I made love to her again, knowing that when it came to her, I would always want more.

MOVEMENT and faint light woke me up. I reached for my sword beside the mattress and pointed to whoever had entered Blair's tent.

"Hey, it's just me," Lennox said, his voice low, and his face turned to the side, so he wasn't looking directly at us.

I lowered the sword and pulled the blankets covering Blair's legs up to her shoulders. She stirred, but didn't wake up.

"What is it?" I asked, disentangling myself from Blair and sitting up. I knew that if Lennox was in here, it was because something that needed my immediate attention happened.

"Can you just get dressed and come to the main tent?" he asked, still staring to the tent's wall. "It's better than facing this lovely orange fabric."

I almost chuckled. "I'll be right there."

Lennox ducked under the tent's entrance flap and left.

And I glanced at the beautiful fae sleeping beside me. A whirlwind of emotions swirled in my chest.

Blair was my mate.

I should have known that from the moment I set eyes on her when we were little kids. Since then, I had been entranced by her. How could anyone else be my mate?

She was not only my soulmate. She was my soul, my heart, my entire life.

I had been a fool by tricking myself into thinking anything else.

But this fact only complicated things further. I didn't want to be crown prince, Blair didn't have an official place in the royal life anymore, and we were practically fighting a war at the moment.

Whatever was happening between Blair and I would have to wait and go slow—if that was possible—because other matters were more urgent and needed my focus right now.

I reached to her and pushed a strand of her hair to the side so I could see her beautiful face before I left. Blair stirred again and peeked at me from under her lashes.

"Sorry," I whispered. "I didn't mean to wake you."

She scooted closer and hooked her arm on my leg. "Are you running away?"

A faint smile spread over my lips. "I'm done running from you."

"Good."

"But Lennox came in. There's a meeting."

Her eyes opened some more. "What happened?"

"I don't know." I leaned over her, placed a kiss on her temple, and stood from the mattress. "But you should rest. I promise that if I need your help, I'll let you know."

"Liar," she said, rolling on the mattress and watching me as I grabbed my clothes and started getting dressed. "If you had your way, you'd lock me in a tower in the middle of a desert island so no one could hurt me."

I nodded. She knew me too well. "Rusting right."

"I can take care of myself."

"I know." I buckled the last of my vest buckles and leaned over her again. "And I gotta say, watching you with a sword is kind of hot."

I kissed her lips, then left the tent before I ended up on the mattress with her again.

The few soldiers around were far from Blair's tent, and Lennox stood halfway to the main tent, waiting for me.

"Where are the other soldiers?"

"Waiting," he said, his voice tight. "We'll get into that." He fell into step with me and smiled. "So, let me guess, you're mates."

I stared at him, dumbfounded. "How did you know?"

He snorted. "You've been in love with her since you were a little kid. That's fate."

I noticed some soldiers glancing from me to Blair's tent. "So, I'm guessing everyone here knows too?"

"Well, not about the mating bond, but they do know you spent the night with Blair. But don't worry, once I saw you going to her, I ordered everyone to step way back. So nobody heard anything."

I scoffed. That was rather thoughtful of my friend. I didn't want anyone else listening to Blair's moans but me.

"Anyway, what's the matter?"

Lennox pressed his mouth tight. We then reached the main tent, he lifted the flap for me. "You'll see."

Frowning, I stepped into the main tent.

General Barric and a handful of soldiers stood around the wooden table, apparently waiting for me.

"Good morning," I muttered, feeling self-conscious—a new one for me.

Lennox snapped his fingers at a scout's face. "Tell him what you told me."

"The sea elves broke the barrier and are advancing toward Coch Caer," the scout said in a rush.

I stilled. "What? Why didn't you wake me earlier?"

"He arrived here fifteen minutes ago," Lennox said. "The moment he told me, I ordered the soldiers to gather and called you."

I glanced around and saw everyone was practically battle ready. All we needed was to get on our horses and leave.

"General Barric," I said. "See to it that enough soldiers are left to defend the camp in case the sea elves decide to surprise us here. We leave in fifteen minutes."

The fae nodded once at me and exited the tent. Lennox turned to me. "You haven't eaten anything since last evening, have you? I'll grab something for you. You eat on the way."

I thanked him as he left, and I turned to the table, where the map was spread out. I glanced at it, at Mor Caer to the north—where the sea elves killed Lugh—and Coch Caer to the south. By the time we got there, the fortress would have fallen, but that didn't mean we wouldn't fight for it. I would do everything I could to take it back.

With a sigh, I walked from the main tent to my tent, where I retrieved my sword, checked if my dagger was secured to my belt, and tightened the buckles of my armor. When I stepped out of my tent, the sun had risen more, illuminating the camp and shining down on the red and orange trees around it, giving them a golden glow. It was the perfect autumn day—not too cold, not too hot, with a soft breeze, and the right amount of sunshine.

All we were missing was some peace.

As I walked toward the edge of the camp, where the soldiers were probably waiting for me, Blair walked out of her tent—in full armor.

I skidded to a stop, then marched to her. She saw me approaching and smiled at me. My sudden anger and the words that were filling my mouth faded when facing her.

She could disarm me with a simple smile.

We stopped a respectable distance from one another, even though all I wanted was to wrap my arm around her waist and pull her to me.

Her smile turned upside down. "Sage came in after you left and told me what was going on."

I eyed her up and down. "And it seems you want to go too."

She frowned. "Don't tell me we have to discuss this again."

I wanted to. I really wanted to, but I knew why she had to do this, why she had to be active and help everyone as much as she could. I admired that about her, and it made me even more proud of her.

This was my rusting mate and she was perfect.

I blew out a long breath. "No, we don't. Just ... stay close to me."

She nodded. "That's even better."

16

BLAIR

WE RODE to Coch Caer in silence. I tried not to think that everyone around us probably knew by now that Red and I had spent the night together. I wanted to hide every time I did. Not because I was embarrassed by my feelings for Red, of being his mate—though I doubted they knew about that—but because until a few days ago, I had been promised to his brother.

That didn't sound good at all.

But I did like the sound of Red being my mate.

I glanced at him, riding by my side, his focus on the road ahead of us. Deep down, I always knew he was the one for me. I had been sure of it when we were younger. We had been best friends, then something else.

When our parents decided on the betrothal, I was ready to join forces with Red and fight for us, but he disappeared. One day he was there, upset about what happened, and the next he was gone. No goodbyes, no notes, no explanations.

Afterward, word reached me that Red, along with Lennox, had joined the army and gone to one of the military training centers, the one farthest from the capital.

I sent a letter to him, one short letter asking him if he was taking the coward's way out, or if he was going to come back and fight for me.

I never received a reply.

I felt angry, betrayed, disappointed, and sad. I held on to those feelings for so long.

At first, it had been hard for me to accept that Lugh, a close friend, would be my husband. I knew he would never be my mate, but I knew that, with time, I might end up loving him as a partner. Together, we would make a good team to lead the kingdom.

Everything had shattered when Lugh died and Red came back.

I couldn't deny that I was glad Red was here. He still made my heart race. He could set me on fire with one touch.

I didn't know what the future held for us, but this time, I hoped he fought for me. I planned to fight for him.

Red raised his hand up high and we slowed down as we turned the last curve in the road and approached the fortress. The gates were open, and a wall of twenty sea elves stood before it. More sea elves hid within the confines of the fortress, probably with bows and arrows ready to lose.

A good distance from the fortress, Red closed his fist and we stopped.

"What's the plan?" I asked as I handed my horse to a lower ranked soldier.

"Brute force," Red said. "We force our way through, kill them all, and take the fortress back."

Red's eyes scanned the walls. I knew he was searching for Ta'hun. I was too. I would give almost anything to exact my revenge against him. But if Ta'hun was here, he was hiding inside Coch Caer.

Our soldiers assembled in groups—the shifters, the ones with magic, the sword fighters, and the archers. Red went with the shifters, and I stayed with the magic group, and even though Sage was a sword fighter, he stayed with me. When Red gave us his signal, he and the others shifted and ran toward the open gates, while the archers struck the sea elves in front and on top of the gates, trying to clear a path for the shifters. The sea elves used shields and walls to protect themselves from the volley, but some weren't as fortunate and were taken down by either arrow or a fox's bite.

The sword fighters followed the foxes in, then it was my group's turn. We advanced, and when we entered the fortress, I was taken aback by how this battle was going. I glanced around—most of the foxes were back in their fae form and fighting along with the sword and magic groups. The bodies of sea elves littered the ground. I thought taking the fortress would be harder.

I didn't have time to dwell on it as a sea elf jumped on

me. I wrapped him with wind and sent him back, slamming him a stone wall. He stayed down. I fought a couple more sea elves, then one of them yelled something in their language and the sea elves ran. Like cowards, they ran from the fortress, retreating.

"Captain Runt, take the foxes, go after them," Red ordered. He was a few feet from me, his armor splashed with blood, his sword's blade red.

Captain Runt dipped his chin, shifted, and pursued the sea elves with the other shifters.

"We should search for surviving fae," I said.

"Right." Red nodded. "Just ... let's be careful. There might be sea elves hiding inside the buildings, and the fae might be ill by now."

General Barric, Captain Omri, and a handful of soldiers turned to check the buildings to our left, while Red, Lennox, Sage, and I entered the administrative building to the right. We cleared halls, offices, and meeting rooms. We found a reinforced door at the end of a corridor a narrow stairwell descended into blackness.

"A prison," Lennox said with a frown. "Does Mor Caer have a prison too?"

Red nodded. "Just a couple of cells, but every fortress and town is required to have somewhere to hold criminals."

Sage grabbed a torch from the wall, Lennox grabbed another, and we went down the dark stairs. The stairs led to a short corridor with eight closed doors. Careful, we opened one by one.

I had opened two and found nothing when I heard a curse word coming from Red in the next cell.

I rushed to him.

And stopped dead on my tracks as soon as I reached the open door.

Beyond it, Red stood frozen in the center of the small, damp cell.

And Lugh sat in the corner.

RED

I STARED AT LUGH. It couldn't be.

But it was.

My heart squeezed as I rushed to him.

"Lugh?" I called as I knelt beside him; he was seated on the cold stone floor, his back and head resting against the rough wall, his eyes closed, his mouth half open. He was filthy and hurt, with his hair looking a crazy mop on his head, and a short beard on his face. Chains wrapped around his wrists and connected to the wall. "Lugh, can you hear me?"

His head lolled forward.

I placed two fingers on his neck, checking for his pulse. It was weak, but it was there.

Lennox burst into the cell and skidded to a stop, his eyes wide. "Red, get away from him! He could be infected!"

I glared at Lennox. "This is my brother. I don't care if he is infected. Find me the rusting keys to the chain before

I break them with my bare hands. And send someone ahead to the camp to have the healer ready for him."

Lennox pressed his lips tight, and I knew he wanted to argue with me. I narrowed my eyes at him, daring him to do so. He knew me well enough to know now wasn't the time to defy me.

Without another word, Lennox whirled on his feet and left.

My eyes shifted from the door to Blair, who was still as a statue inside the cell, her hands over her mouth, her eyes bulged.

I knew what she was feeling. Relief that he was alive, but worry. What would become of us now that Lugh was back? I shook my head and focused on my brother. I would worry about that later. Now, I had to make sure he was well.

Blair dropped to her knees. "I thought ... I thought he had died." Her eyes filled with tears. "I left him behind because I thought he had died. If I had known ... I would have fought harder for him."

I frowned. Guilt—I knew that feeling well.

"Don't worry, Blair," I said, turning my attention back to Lugh. "We'll get him out of here and he'll be all right."

At least, that was what I was praying for.

IT DIDN'T TAKE LONG for Lennox to come back with the keys. We unchained Lugh and I picked him up in my arms

—a lot lighter than I thought he would be. The sea elves starved him, and he was now skin and bones.

Word spread among the soldiers and the fortress's residents that Lugh was alive as I carried him out of the fortress and put him on my horse. We rode back slowly, because I didn't want to jostle him and make him suffer more than he already had.

The healer waited for us on the edge of the camp. I carried Lugh to my tent, with the healer right beside me, already checking Lugh's vitals.

Blair, Lennox, General Barric, and Sage entered the tent with us, but they kept to the back, away from the mattress where I laid Lugh's frail body, in case the healer needed space to work.

The healer's hands trembled as he examined Lugh.

I sat beside them and waited patiently, but after a few minutes of tense silence, I finally said, "Talk to me."

"I'm just starting, my prince," the healer said, his voice low. "But from the little I'm seeing, I can say the crown prince is definitely dehydrated, malnourished, and some of his wounds are infected."

"What about the sea plague?" Lennox asked from behind me. I whipped my head fast and shot him a glare. He ignored me.

"I-I need a little longer to determine that," the healer answered.

The flap of the tent opened wide, and a woman with long black hair stepped in. "Back away from him," Mahaeru said, her voice firm. The healer jumped several feet back and bowed low to the goddess. I didn't move. She fixed her dark eyes on me. "Prince Redlen," she said, her words a warning.

Lennox clasped a hand around my shoulder and tugged hard. I wanted to defy a goddess, but I knew why she was here. I knew why she was asking us to stay away from Lugh.

Without taking my eyes from Mahaeru, I let Lennox pull me back. "He has the sea plague," I said.

Mahaeru nodded. "I'm afraid so."

"We still have to treat him," Blair said, her first words since we found Lugh at the fortress. "He's weak, in need of nourishment and care."

"True." The goddess glanced at Blair. "That's why you'll take him to the capital and treat him there. Maehara will be there shortly and will warn Princess Maize. She'll ready Prince Lugh's chambers to receive him, along with a healer who has more knowledge about the plague."

"True, my goddess," the healer said. "I don't know much about the sea plague." The healer lifted his eyes to me, apologetically. "I'm a battle healer, my prince. I stop bleedings and close wounds. Nothing more."

I glared at him, ready to take someone's head off. But the poor healer wasn't to blame. No one was. I let out a long breath. I had a battle to fight, enemies to defeat. I couldn't be coming and going from Masarn all the time.

But this was Lugh … my brother, the true crown prince. He deserved my attention, more than anyone.

"All right, we leave for the capital in thirty minutes."

18

BLAIR

BEING BACK at the Oren Palace should have been a moment of celebration. It should have meant we defeated the sea elves and our beautiful kingdom was safe. It wasn't supposed to be like this—locked in my usual guest bedroom like a prisoner.

I paced, my boots clicking on the stone floors, my hands twisting on themselves, worry and tension creating knots inside of me.

But I wasn't the only one in isolation. Since Mahaeru first told us about Lugh having the sea plague, we all kept our distance, even when riding to Masarn. Upon arrival, the soldiers were sent to the barracks, where they were quarantined in their rooms, and Red was locked in his chambers. We were all under observation since we had been in close contact with not only Lugh, but also the sea elves and the fortress's residents.

Since finding Lugh in the fortress, Red had not spoken to me directly, and barely looked my way.

I wasn't sure how he felt, but I had an inkling that it couldn't be different than the storm swirling in my chest. There was too much going on, and it was hard to make sense of it all.

Our first priority should be to get the plague under control and defeat our enemies. But there was also Lugh, the lost crown prince, who had returned from the dead.

And the fact that my betrothal to him was probably still standing, even though I was mated to his brother.

I buried my face in my hands.

I stilled.

Slowly, I pressed my palm to my forehead.

Sure enough, I was running a fever.

THE IDEA of escaping from my chambers crossed my mind more than I would like to admit, but I knew I shouldn't do that. If I was sick too, I would only be putting others at risk.

I received reports every hour.

Lugh's health—he was still weak and unconscious. The healer had been administering the only medicine we had against the sea plague, but it was never effective. It helped with pain and slowed the virus, but it didn't truly stop it. The plague was fatal.

The quarantine situation—at least half of the fae from the fortress and the soldiers who had fought in the battle were now showing symptoms of the sea plague, like fever and headache. I kept praying it was a fluke and none of them were really sick.

The camp and the barrier—though days had passed since we took Coch Maer back, the sea elves hadn't tried anything else. They were on the beach, enjoying the sand and the sea, while we scrambled to save fae from a fatal illness.

Which brought me to an ugly conclusion: This was their plan all along. That was why they hadn't fought us, why they hadn't pushed back and come at us with all they had. In the beginning of our history, many eons ago, when the sea elves started coming for our lands, they didn't know about the sea plague. Neither did we. It took our ancestors many years and invasions for them to link the sea plague to the sea elves. Back then, the plague was called something else. But with time, they learned about it just as we did, and each time they came and we defeated them, we were left with a relentless wave of sickness that we had to contain.

It seemed that the sea elves had become too smart for their own good. This time, they attacked us long enough to spread the illness. Now, all they needed to do was sit back and relax while the illness spread and killed us. Even if it didn't kill all of us, it would take many lives, weakening the kingdom. Making it easier for them to take over.

That knowledge, that fact killed me.

The other thing that killed me was this whole situation with Blair and Lugh, this inevitable triangle we were wrapped in. Though I was praying for a miracle, Lugh wouldn't survive the virus, but having him alive, even if for a little while, made me feel guilty. I had mated his fiancée. How crazy was that? How did we solve that problem? We didn't. What I did was lock all my feelings and thoughts about that situation in the depths of my soul. This wasn't the time to worry about that.

Finally, after two days of agonizing inside my rusting room, the healer came to check on me as he did several times a day, but his news was different.

"I'm glad to say you're healthy, Prince Redlen." He sounded relieved. "You don't have the sea plague. You may leave your chambers now."

I let out a long sigh. "Thank the chilly wind." It was hard to run a kingdom and organize a war from inside four walls. I picked up my vest and headed to Lugh's chambers.

The double doors were open and a heavy curtain fell over the opening. I pulled the curtain to the side and glanced—Lugh was in his bed on the other side of the room, and the windows beside it were wide open, airing the room so the virus wouldn't easily spread.

Even from here, I could see the slow rise and fall of his chest. He was still alive. I closed my eyes and prayed, *render us a miracle. Let him live.*

Things between Blair, Lugh, and me would be difficult, but we would deal with it. It would be better that than losing my brother all over again.

The healer stopped a foot behind me. "He's a fighter. The illness is trying to take him, but Prince Lugh is fighting."

I frowned. That was good, but I hated that he was suffering. Again, I wished for a miracle. "If anyone can beat this, it's Lugh."

Though we all knew no one could beat this.

"Prince Redlen," the healer said, his voice low. I looked at him. "There's something else you should know."

ONCE THE FEVER STARTED, things went downhill fast. I couldn't tell the difference between day and night, and I spent most of the time in my bed, sleeping and dreaming —nightmares of monsters attacking the Oren Palace and killing every fae in the Autumn Court.

The healer checked on me every few hours, and one of his assistants came even more often. My parents also came every day, along with Jora, even though I had asked them not to. My mother had practically fainted and her sobs upset me more than helped. I also didn't like them coming and going when so many people around the palace were in quarantine. Though I knew everyone was being extra careful, this plague was tricky. I would rather they stayed safe in our house, away from the palace.

Maize and Willow also came to visit a couple of times each day. They stayed by the door, as the healer had instructed, and whenever possible, they only withdrew the curtain placed there for a few minutes at a time. Though my bed had been moved closer to the windows, and they remained open all the time, even at night when it got chilly. I didn't want to risk having anyone being infected because of me.

This particular afternoon, I was tired, the fever and the chills unrelenting, but I felt a tiny bit better, enough to prop my pillows up and sit on the bed instead of cowering under the blankets and hoping to sleep.

As I closed my eyes, I saw movement behind the curtain. A moment later, the curtains were pulled aside and Willow's smiling face greeted me.

"You look better," the young fae said. "Are you taking the medicine?"

I gestured to the side table, where a tray full of untouched food and drinks sat along with the medicine. "Yes," I told her. Though I wasn't sure why I was even taking it. To help with the pain, to make my death slower? Wouldn't it be better to get this misery over with?

"You know, I think I had an idea—"

"Blair," a voice boomed from the hallway. A wide-eyed Red appeared beside Willow. His eyes locked with mine and my heart lurched. "No, no, no," he whispered.

A faint smile stretched over my lips. "You're all right." I pressed a hand to my chest. "Thank the red leaves."

"But you aren't." He took a step forward, in my bedroom, and I sat straighter.

"Stop! Stay back!" I shouted. He took another step. "Red! I'll call the guards. Stay back!"

He halted, his hands up. "I just ... I can't ..." His eyes shone with unshed tears.

My heart squeezed again. I knew what he was feeling, because if I was in his shoes, I would be feeling the same. He was my mate and I was his. It hurt him to see me like this. Oh by the chilly wind, how I wished I could ease his pain.

"I'm fine," I assured him. "It's ... slow and it doesn't hurt much, thanks to the medicine."

"First Lugh, now you." He shook his head. "I can't take this. I'm going to call Mahaeru. I'll make a deal with her. If she heals you both, I'll ... I don't know—"

"Don't talk nonsense," I snapped. That was so like Red, wanting to save others by sacrificing himself. "You won't do anything that foolish."

"I have an idea," Willow said, her voice louder than usual. Red turned to her and she cowered under his inquisitive gaze. "Hm, remember Bloodwrath? The witch Layla?"

"King Varian's mate," I whispered, recalling her. "Yes, I remember her. What about her?"

"She's powerful and really good with potions," Willow continued. "I was thinking that maybe if you ask her to take a look at the medicine you have available and ask her to improve on it, maybe even use her magic to shift it into a potion that will heal those infected with the sea plague ..."

Red's eyes returned to mine. "That isn't a bad idea," he whispered.

"No, it's not," I agreed.

Red pressed his lips tight. "I'll see to this. Meanwhile, you rest and do whatever the healer asks of you."

I nodded. "Yes, my prince."

He glared at me for a moment, before turning around and taking Willow by the hand. "All right, you're going to help me. Let's go."

WITH PERFECT TIMING, Mahaeru showed up as I was about to order a page to get my horse ready. Other than riding as fast as the wind, there was no other way to get to the Summer Court.

Until Mahaeru opened a portal right into the heart of the Sun City. The fae here might not know me well enough, but they knew the goddess. Once the soldiers at the palace gates saw her, they ushered her in.

King Varian and Queen Layla met us in the grand hall. The last time I had seen both was almost a year ago, when I had come to help them defeat the witch Sanna and her ogres. The only thing that had changed since then was the golden crowns on their heads.

"That chair suits you," I teased as Varian rose from his throne to greet me.

He clasped his arm with mine, holding on tight. "I've heard what's happening. I'm so sorry."

I nodded. "Thank you." I turned to Layla and she offered me a small smile. Her blond hair matched the shine from the crown. "I think you can help us."

"With what?"

I fished a small vial from my pocket. "This is the medicine we use to slow the spread of the sea plague and lessen the suffering of those afflicted. I think that with your expertise and magic, you might be able to make it more effective."

She took the vial from me and lifted it to her eye level. "You want me to make it better, like ... you want me to transform this into a cure."

It was not a question. "I want you to at least try."

Layla wrapped her hand around the vial and glanced at Mahaeru. She opened her mouth, but closed it when the goddess turned her hand, revealing a golden ring with a red stone. "You'll need it."

"I know," Layla whispered. With trembling fingers, she took the ring. "But you'll come back to get it once I'm done, right?"

"I'll be with you the entire way," Mahaeru said, her tone firm. "When you're done, I'll take the ring and the cure from you."

The goddess's words weren't lost on me. "Did you say a cure? So you know Layla will succeed?"

Mahaeru shot me an annoyed glance. "Patience, Prince Redlen."

Patience? While my brother, my mate, and many other fae were dying? That was not only hard, but impossible.

"I should be able to do it, but it'll take a while," Layla said. "A couple of days, at least."

Varian grasped my shoulder. "You're welcome to stay while you wait."

I shook my head. "I appreciate the offer, but I need to go back. There's much to do."

"I understand." Varian dropped his hand.

I thanked them profusely, a relieved sensation skirting around me, but I didn't let it get too close. It was too soon for that.

Mahaeru opened the portal for me again, but she didn't come with me this time. Alone, I crossed over and went to work.

FOR THE NEXT couple of days, I busied myself like I had never done before. I sent scouts to check on the camp and the barrier often, and I also received reports throughout the day. The sea elves had not moved, which only reinforced my idea that they were waiting for the right time to attack.

I also visited the many improvised shelters and tents outside Masarn, where the evacuated fae and the sick fae were being kept. I brought them clothes, food, toys for the young ones, and able hands to help out. Healers I had sent days ago treated the sick fae and made sure they were isolated.

The fae thanked me profusely, and the healthy ones

held on to my hands, as if I could help them more with a simple touch.

It broke my heart to see what had happened to my kingdom, how deep it had fallen, but there was hope on the horizon. Layla would be able to make a cure, and soon everyone, including Blair and Lugh, would be better.

Which brought on more problems, but I shut those thoughts before they began. It wasn't worth it to dwell on them yet.

I also visited Lugh and Blair either late at night when I was about to turn in, or early morning, when I woke up before the sun was up. Lugh was barely conscious. Just once he was awake and recognized me. "The rebel prince is back," he said, before falling asleep again.

Blair didn't seem well either. Her health was deteriorating fast, despite the medicine, and I hadn't seen her awake, though Willow assured me she had lucid moments during the day.

Two days passed, then three, then four ... and Layla still had not sent Mahaeru with the cure. I was starting to think it hadn't really worked, when finally, on the sixth day after I had asked the new queen of the Summer Court for a favor, a portal opened up in one of the Oren Palace's courtyards, right when I was walking around it, trying to clear my head.

Mahaeru and Layla crossed the portal. Smiling, Layla approached me. She handed me a vial with a dark green liquid. "Here. This should work." I took the vial from her.

"You should test it. In case it doesn't work, I can make tweaks."

I closed my hand around the vial and held it dearly. "Thank you."

"Don't thank me yet," she said. "Now, who will be our first volunteer?"

BLAIR

As the days passed, I got worse and worse. I didn't know how many days were gone, but Willow and Maize told me each time they came to visit. I promptly forgot, along with everything else they said. It was becoming harder and harder to hold on to sanity and consciousness. All I wanted to do was sleep.

But I was afraid that one of these days, I wouldn't wake up again.

Though they tried keeping sad news from me, I demanded to know what was happening—many fae had already died from the sea plague, Lugh was still alive but in worse shape than I was, and Red was going crazy, waiting for Layla and the new medicine.

When Willow told me Layla and Mahaeru had arrived and needed a volunteer, I offered myself.

"No," Red said from my chamber's entrance. He

crossed his arms and hid the vial he was holding. "No way."

Beside him, Layla seemed a little uncomfortable with the whole situation.

Ignoring Red, Mahaeru walked into the bedroom and approached my bed. I scooted as far as I could. "Don't worry. I can't get infected." She extended her hand, producing another vial. "I knew he wouldn't agree, so I brought an extra."

I glanced at Red—his tanned face paled. Gingerly, I took the vial, uncapped it, and drank the bitter liquid before he could protest.

Immediately, my stomach turned and I pressed a hand to it, sure I would throw up.

"That's part of it," Layla said, her tone low. "Sorry I couldn't make it more pleasant."

"It's okay," I croaked. I took deep breaths through my mouth. Even if this was a magical potion, it wouldn't work in a few seconds, would it?

Without taking her eyes from me, Mahaeru said, "Willow, call the healer."

The young fae dashed down the hallway.

Red stiffened. "Why? What's happening?"

"Relax, Prince Redlen," Mahaeru said. "We need him to confirm if the new medicine is working or not."

The healer was probably busy on the other side of the palace, tending to the sick fae who actually needed his immediate attention, and yet, he had been called for one of the noble ladies. If this wasn't for a good cause, for something that could possibly heal us all, I would have refused. His time was better spent helping others, not me.

The minutes ticked by. Red paced the wide corridor outside, Layla stood quiet under the doorjamb, and Mahaeru looked like a statue seated at the edge of my bed.

I closed my eyes, trying to feel everything. Was it working? Was the fever reducing? Was the pain lessening? I couldn't tell, not yet.

Something tugged in my stomach. It turned again and I pressed a hand over my mouth. Pain bloomed along with it, spreading fast and taking me like a storm.

My hands trembled and dark spots danced in my visions.

Red halted at the doorway. "Blair, what's wrong?"

The pain exploded and I couldn't hold it anymore. A scream ripped from my throat and I fell back on the mattress.

I TOOK A STEP FORWARD. Mahaeru pointed a finger at me. "Stay right there, Prince Redlen."

I pressed my lips together, clenching my teeth and my fists. How did the goddess want me to stay back when Blair was writhing in her bed, suffering.

"This ... this shouldn't be happening," Layla said, her eyes wide.

This was her fault!

I stopped that thought before it took root. It wasn't her fault. It was mine. I had agreed to Willow's idea, I had gone after Layla, and I had believed in the goddess when she seemed so sure this would work.

And now Blair was paying for it.

Blair gasped and stilled.

I lurched forward. In a flash, Mahaeru appeared in front of me. "She's fine."

I blinked. "What?" I glanced over the goddess's shoulders. In her bed, Blair sat up. "What's going on?"

She pressed a hand to her forehead. "My fever seems to have broken." She glanced at her hands. "I'm not trembling anymore." She looked at me, a faint smile on her lips. "My vision isn't blurred either." She inhaled deeply. "And my mind feels clear."

Layla clapped her hands. "It's working."

The rush of footsteps down the hall made me turn to the door. The healer ran into the room, with Willow at his heels. The young fae stopped by the door with Layla, but the healer kept on going until he was beside Blair.

"How do you feel?" he asked, examining her.

"A little tired, hungry and thirsty, but other than that, I feel fine," Blair said, her voice light. "Better than I have felt in several days."

After a few tense minutes during which the healer examined Blair's skin, her eyes, and even took some of her blood and mixed it with some magical reagent, the healer finally stood and grinned at us. "She's cured."

My knees wobbled with relief. "Are you sure?"

The healer nodded. "There are no traces of the virus in her blood."

I sidestepped the goddess, and in three long steps, reached Blair's bed. I practically threw myself over her, the bed groaning with the sudden extra weight. I heard hushed voices as the others were ushered out of the bedroom by the goddess, but that was all I noticed, because the rest of my attention was on the fae in my arms.

I held her tight against me. "I thought I would lose you."

"For a moment there, I thought so too." She buried her face on my neck and inhaled deeply. "It's good to hold you like this." Then she pulled back. "But we have work to do."

"Wait, what?"

As if she hadn't been on her deathbed a second ago, Blair stood from the bed. "We need to take the cure to the other fae, to Lugh." She took a step and lost her footing.

"Whoa." Standing beside her, I caught her elbow and kept her from falling to the floor. "I don't want to argue, but I think you have to take it slow."

"I'm fine." She pressed a hand to my chest. "Just a little weak from being in my bed for days. I'll get dressed, eat and drink something, and then I'm going to work. And you can't stop me."

Blair headed to the door that led to her closet. Although this was just her guest bedroom, which she rarely used, it was filled with many of her things.

I let out a sigh. "I know that, but you can't expect me not to worry."

She spied me from the door. "As long as you don't stop me, I don't mind you worrying."

I shook my head. Yes, I was worried, but that was one of the reasons I loved her so much. Even when she was ill, Blair wouldn't stop if she could help our people.

If only everyone was as selfless and caring as she was …

THE DAY WAS busy and fast. After confirming the cure worked, Layla went back to the Summer Court to finish making more. She assured us it would only take a couple of hours to brew them and have hundreds of doses ready. Meanwhile, Lennox, Maize, Willow, and I organized the sick fae, so we could deliver the cure to them faster. Despite the healer's recommendations to take it slow, Blair ignored him and joined us. The fae were overjoyed to see her well again. It gave them hope, which meant the world right now.

Later in the day, Layla, Varian, and a handful of their soldiers brought over dozens of boxes filled with vials—the cure.

I clasped Varian's arm. "I don't know if I'll ever be able to repay you for this."

Varian shook his head. "First, you already helped us when we were battling Sanna. Second, we are doing this because we want to."

I hugged Layla and thanked her too. She said she would stay on standby, in case something went wrong, or unexpected side effects showed up. "Just send Mahaeru to get me."

"Will do," I assured her. "Thank you again."

They left, and we worked nonstop until every sick fae had received the cure, taken it, and started showing signs of being healed. Some experienced the same pain and discomfort that Blair had, but most didn't.

Then, Blair and I took the cure to Lugh.

The healer had to open my brother's mouth and pour

the cure inside, as he was unconscious, his fever high. According to the healer, without the cure, Lugh might have lasted another day or two, at most.

I held Blair's hand as we waited across the room, our eyes fixed on Lugh.

Finally, after what seemed an eternity, Lugh took in a deep breath, opened his eyes, and sat up in bed. "What is going?" he asked, looking around. He saw me and frowned. "The rebel prince is back?"

I chuckled. He had said that to me already, but he had been so out of it, he hadn't remembered. Self-conscious, I let go of Blair's hand and approached his bed. "How are you feeling?"

"Like I had to hike over the mountains, naked and weaponless, with a pack of wild wolves on my ass." The color was returning to his cheeks, along with his dry humor. "I don't remember much, though I know the sea elves captured me and I was sick with the plague." He frowned. "How am I feeling better now?"

I sat on the bed beside him and started telling him all I knew. Meanwhile, Blair called the healer to check on the crown prince, and had nourishment brought to his chambers. Maize and Willow also came to see him, and later Maize brought our mother with her. Queen Aurelia seemed in better spirits with her three children under her wings.

At that time, Blair called on Willow and the two exited the chambers, leaving us alone.

Because Lugh had been on his deathbed, he was too

weak to stand or even to speak for long, so he remained in bed while we had supper with him in his chambers. It felt awkward and forced, but at the same time, it was nice. It was like we were children again. All we were missing was our father.

THAT NIGHT, I couldn't sleep.

There was too much in my mind and no clear path ahead of me.

Lugh was too weak and would be so for a few more days, which meant he couldn't simply stand and lead us to battle against the sea elves.

He was alive, which meant he was still the crown prince, and Blair was still his betrothed.

And she was still my mate.

I stood at an open window at my chambers, looking out at the city below, at the twinkling lights from the few alight windows and street lamps, giving a warm glow to the night. Above, the dark skies were dotted with millions of stars, the moon a crescent line on the horizon.

Behind me, the door opened, and I knew who it was without looking. I could sense her, where she was and went, as if there was a line connecting us, letting me know how far or close she was to me, ever since the mating bond snapped.

I wanted to reach for her, to embrace her, to hold on to

me, to kiss her, to take her to my bed ... but it felt wrong. Even though she was mine, it was wrong now.

I stood my ground as Blair walked closer and halted by my side, her face turned forward too.

"How are you doing?" she asked, her words almost a whisper lost in the night.

I sighed. "I don't know," I confessed. If she had asked me this question two weeks ago, I would have said it wasn't her business. But things had changed since then. "I feel lost."

She nodded. "I understand. I feel like I'm in a whirlpool, sinking faster and faster. I can only imagine it's worse for you."

It was bad for both of us. Though I was the one pushing the kingdom forward now, trying to lead it and help it, Blair's responsibilities didn't fall far behind mine. She was once more the future queen, after all.

And that was one of the reasons why I wanted to deal with our situation last. "My priority is our enemies," I told her, though, deep down, I knew that was me trying to convince myself of the right course of action.

She nodded again.

We stayed quiet for a little while, standing side by side, watching the stars twinkling in the night sky, taking comfort in each other's company.

"Red," Blair whispered, breaking the silence. I glanced at her. "About the sea elves ..."

I turned, giving her my full attention. "Yes?"

A half-smile pulled at her lips. "I have a plan."

RED PUT my plan into action at once. He didn't even sleep that night. Me neither, for that matter. We started working right away, turning my plan into a reality so we could win this thing.

The shelters outside Masarn were moved farther into the kingdom, but the tents and belongings remained. The entirety of Masarn was evacuated too, making the capital look like a ghost town. Maize, the queen, and Lugh didn't want to leave the palace, but besides looking convincing, we had to keep them safe. Lugh argued he wanted to fight, but when Red put a sword in his hand so he could prove he wouldn't be a liability, Lugh could barely hold it. Between almost dying of his injuries during that first battle and the illness, Lugh was still too weak. But he was healing more and more every day. With time, he would be fine.

When everyone was gone and ready, Red summoned

the soldiers stationed near the coast. They abandoned the camp, and even the soldiers forming the barrier retreated.

All of this took a few days, but Red and I knew we had a little time. After all, the sea elves were waiting for the illness to take us all, weren't they?

Finally, after three days of calling back the soldiers, our scouts sent news: the sea elves were on the move. We made one last sweep through Masarn and the Oren Palace, made sure the houses were empty and that all fae were safe, then we waited.

In an unusually gray day, chillier than most, we saw them advancing to Masarn's gates, as if they owned the place. They thought that by now, we had all been infected and died. Or the vast majority of our population had. They thought they wouldn't have to fight us. All they had to do was to take.

They stomped into the capital. A few sea elves ran ahead, entering houses or other buildings, searching for life. There was none—we were hidden in attics and on rooftops, where they couldn't see us.

Beside me, Red watched from a blurred window on the last floor of one of the tallest buildings, one close to the inner gate that led to the palace. We had a handful of soldiers with us, as there were others in similar positions around town, but most of the soldiers were beyond the inner walls, waiting for our signal.

We saw the sea elves advancing, their leaders at the front of the line. When they crossed the inner gates, which shut closed behind them, leaving the majority of their soldiers behind.

Chaos ensued.

The sea elves on this side of the gates roared. They thrust their weapons at the gates, trying to break them. Some tried scaling it, others ran along the walls, trying to find a weak point.

"It's time," Red said. He turned to me, the small coin Mahaeru had given to him in his hand. He pressed the coin between two fingers and a portal opened. It was a one-time thing, according to the goddess.

The soldiers went through first, then me, and lastly Red.

We exited on the front steps of the palace, with the courtyard open wide before us—and the Autumn soldiers surrounding two dozen confused sea elves.

From the other side of the inner wall, we heard the confusion of the sea elves, and the insistent thud of an improvised battering ram.

Chest puffed, Red approached them.

I trailed behind him.

"You tricked us," one of the sea elves said through gritted teeth, his accent thick. By the looks of his armor and his stance, he wasn't one of the chiefs. He was the leader—Su'jin. He took a few steps forward, but the tips of the spears our soldiers held stopped him. "Well played."

"Surrender," Red said.

Su'jin chuckled. "Or what? You think you can defeat us?"

"I know I can," Red answered, serious.

Su'jin's eyes flared. "I want to see you try."

A wicked grin adorned Red's lips. "My pleasure."

I WALKED CLOSER to the circle of fae who surrounded the sea elves in the palace's front courtyard.

The soldiers stepped to the side, creating a space wide enough for me to walk through. Su'jin narrowed his eyes and lifted his axe. If he attacked me now, he would be dead in seconds; he was smart enough to know that. I could see it in his eyes, how he calculated the odds of killing me before the others could kill him. But what good would that do? The other sea elves would be killed in seconds too, and after we defeated the leaders, I was sure we could subdue the ones on the other side of the inner wall too.

Su'jin held his ground. "What are you doing?"

"Showing you this." I fished a small vial from my vest pocket and showed it to him. "This is a serum designed to kill your kind in matters of seconds."

Su'jin balked. "You're bluffing."

"Would you like a demonstration?" I snapped my fingers.

Lennox and General Barric came forward and grabbed one of them—the sea elf who had almost killed Lugh and Blair. Ta'hun. I had no idea of the exact rankings of the sea elves, but I knew this particular sea elf ranked directly below Su'jin.

Ta'hun struggled against Lennox and General Barric's hold, shouting in his language, probably asking for Su'jin to help him. But Su'jin ignored him. Sage approached the group and helped Lennox and General Barric. The three of them subdued Ta'hun, forcing him to kneel. Sage held his hair and pulled his head back. The sea elf screamed. Before he knew what was happening, I uncapped the vial and poured the liquid into his mouth.

Ta'hun spit it out, but I was sure most of it had gone down his throat. He was done for.

Lennox, General Barric, and Sage let go of Ta'hun and stepped back. The sea elf's body started trembling. "What's happening?" he asked, his eyes wide. He fell forward to the ground, his body convulsing.

"Look!" Another sea elf pointed to the one writhing on the ground. His skin darkened and smoked, as if he was being burned from the inside. They all retreated, as if it was contagious. It wasn't, but they didn't need to know that.

Ta'hun stilled, his eyes wide, his mouth open, his body limp.

All of this had been Blair's idea. Pretending most of us had been infected and died or gotten so sick, we couldn't fight. Making the capital look like a ghost town, as if we were already dead. Hiding the soldiers and waiting. Asking Layla to create a serum fatal to the sea elves, but harmless to us.

Despite the dark side of her plan, I had never been prouder of Blair. She alone could lead this kingdom and this army. She didn't need a male fae by her side.

I lifted the empty vial. "I have thousands of doses more. I can dip them on arrows and our blades and kill you all."

Su'jin glanced from the dead body to me. From the dead body to me, several times. "What do you want?"

I took another step closer. "I want you to leave my land and never come back." I showed him the vial again. "If you do, we'll be waiting. The next time, you won't make it two steps onto our beaches before we kill you all."

Su'jin stared at me, probably trying to find the bluff in my words. There was none. As much as it sickened me to have picked Ta'hun and killed him—I would rather it had been during a fair fight—it was a necessary evil. If I wanted to avoid hundreds of more deaths, I had to do this. I had to show them we were as ruthless as they were.

Another sea elf approached Su'jin and whispered in his ear.

A moment later, Su'jin nodded at me. "Fine," he barked, clearly unhappy. "We'll leave."

"And never come back," I added.

Su'jin hesitated. "We'll leave and never come back."

"Good." I suppressed a sigh of relief. I didn't want to show them any sign of weakness or compassion, but I was truly glad he had taken the deal as I was tired of bloody battles. I prayed he kept his word and I never had to use the serum. "We'll escort you back to your ships."

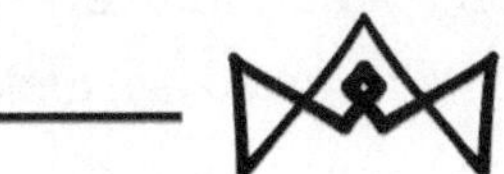

RED and our soldiers disarmed the sea elves and bound them with reinforced ropes and chains, then escorted them to the coast. I stayed in the capital to help the fae return to their houses and stores. The fae who had camped outside the capital were instructed to remain there for a few more days, to give Red time to send the sea elves away.

I also helped out at the palace since Queen Aurelia was still a little out of it, Lugh too weak, Maize didn't have one diplomatic bone in her body, and Willow was too young.

An entire week passed. The fae in the camps left, the soldiers stationed in the capital returned to the garrison, Lugh felt stronger every day, but Red hadn't returned.

I was giving him the benefit of the doubt. He hadn't sent one letter, one response. I imagined he was riding up and down the coast, scouring every inch of land and ocean, making sure all of the sea elves were really gone.

Otherwise, why hadn't he come back yet? I didn't allow

myself to go down that path. I held on to the belief he was still out there, taking care of our kingdom and our safety. Soon, he would return to the Oren Palace.

Right?

When the second week came and went, my faith in him started failing. I asked General Barric and other soldiers about his whereabouts, and everyone gave me the same answer: Red had stayed to make sure everything was all right, but he sent the soldiers back to their posts.

So, I had been right.

I held on to that until a third week passed. Then, despite being busy with royal life, I started unraveling.

The worst moment was when Queen Aurelia invited us for tea. It felt like we had skipped the last few weeks and were back to before the sea elves invasion, Lugh's near death, Red's comeback, and the mating bond. Even my mother had been invited, to her delight.

Queen Aurelia's head was worse than ever.

"Lugh, my dear, you're looking so gaunt," she said with a soft smile. "Have you been eating well?"

My chest squeezed. Queen Aurelia didn't remember that the sea elves had been at her doorstep mere weeks ago. She didn't remember we had a ceremony to mourn Lugh's death, and that Red had been here, running things as best as he could under the circumstances. She didn't remember we had found Lugh alive, but ill with the sea plague, that the palace had been quarantined, that I had been sick too, and everything else after that. I was glad she didn't remember our suffering and our worry, but I didn't like seeing her unraveling like this.

Lugh glanced at me, seated by my side, then at Maize, who often had unshed tears in her eyes. The crown prince cleared his throat before smiling at his mother. "Yes, Mother. I'm eating well."

"Then, when will we have the wedding?" she asked.

It was like a punch to my gut. Since Lugh's recovery, we hadn't talked about our betrothal. We skirted the subject while working to get the kingdom back on its feet.

Beside me, Lugh shifted his weight, visibly bothered by the question.

"Oh, Queen Aurelia," my mother started, surprising me. "There is still much to do after all that fighting and the illness."

The queen narrowed her eyes at my mother. "Fighting? Illness?"

"Mother!" I hissed.

My mother put a hand over her mouth and stared at me, her eyes huge. "Sorry," she mouthed.

"Nothing, Mother." Maize took her mother's hand and patted it. "It's nothing. Would you like more tea?" She reached for the teapot, but her handmaid stepped up and did it for her.

But that had done the trick. The queen's fragile mind shifted to the tea and biscuits, and she forgot about the fighting and the illness once more.

The rest of the afternoon was tense and long. Finally, when it was time to leave, Lugh called me to talk to him.

My mother and Jora went ahead to the carriage and waited for me—I had returned to my parents' house now that everything was back to normal—and I followed Lugh to the gallery, where several oil portraits of his ancestors in gilded frames adorned the walls.

In the center of the room, Lugh turned to me. He looked much better since he was cured from the sea plague. His eyes were warm and his smile was kind, but there was a hollow in cheeks that wasn't there before, and his skin seemed pale. The healer had told us he might not be as strong as before, but he was healthy. That was all that mattered.

"It seems the rebel prince left again," Lugh said.

I frowned, wondering where he was going with this subject. "I don't think he likes to be called that."

"I know, but you can't deny it fits him right. Once again, he left without a word, like a ghost."

"I'm sure he has his reasons," I said, my tone snappier than I would like. Why was I defending Red? He didn't deserve my protection.

"Blair," Lugh started, his voice low. Even though no one seemed to be around, we both knew we were never truly alone. "I've been avoiding this conversation, but it's only causing us more pain."

I frowned. "What are you talking about?"

He let out a long sigh. "Redlen is your mate, isn't he?"

I stilled. My first instinct was to deny it, but where that would lead me? This was Lugh, one of my oldest friends, and someone I cared about too much. "Yes, he is."

"I knew it." He clasped his hands behind his back. "To be honest, I thought Redlen and you would be mates since we were young. Anyone could see how he looked at you, how the two of you seemed to gravitate to each other. It was hard not to see it." He pressed his lips together. "But when our parents arranged for our betrothal, I was blind-sided. I wasn't expecting it, and it took me a long time to react to it. By then, Redlen was already gone."

That was a surprise. "You tried to break the betrothal?"

Lugh nodded. "I did, but our parents were enamored with the idea. And ... I confess that after Red left and we began spending time together, I understood their decision. Don't get me wrong. As much as I hoped to fall in love with you and you with me, that didn't happen, but I could see how well we worked together, how much you cared for the kingdom, for our fae. You would make a fabulous queen."

Despite everything, I felt warmth spreading over my cheeks. I hadn't expected a compliment from Lugh, or anyone else for that matter.

But his words weren't lost in me. "You said would make ... what do you mean?"

"I can't force you to marry me, Blair. Because let's face it, it was a deal between our parents, not us. We are older now, wiser I hope, and we don't need to do this to ourselves." He took a step closer and held one of my hands in between his. "I have immense respect for you. I'm honored to have you as my fiancée, and I do love you, but as a friend, a partner, an equal. Just not as a lover. I don't want you to marry me if you would rather be with Red."

My chest squeezed, then expanded and I took in a deep breath. I felt the same way. "Thank you for taking my opinion and my feelings into consideration." Because our parents and the council didn't care about my opinions or feelings. I held his hands tight. "I want to work for the good of our kingdom. I know I can do more for our fae, but …"

"I understand." He nodded. "Let me assure you of one thing: You might not become queen, Blair, but you'll always have a place here. In fact, I'll make you a royal advisor. An official title to go with all I know you can still do for the Autumn Court."

I smiled. "I like that."

"I knew you would."

I withdrew my hands from his. "What about you? What will you do?"

Lugh squared his shoulders. "I'll run this country. I might even talk to my mother and convince her to pass the crown. It's time for her to rest. Meanwhile, I'll keep my eyes and my heart open, and hopefully one day I'll also find my mate and I'll make her my queen."

I liked that idea. "I'll cheer when that happens."

"Thanks." He stared into my eyes. "What will you do now?"

I shrugged. "I'm not sure, but when I find your brother, I'm going to kick his ass."

A loud laugh bubbled past Lugh's lips. "I would like to see that."

I HAD LOST my mind there for a moment.

Like a coward, I had left the Oren Palace once more. Holding on to the excuse of escorting the sea elves back to their ships, I stayed back and didn't return. At first, I told myself I was making sure all the sea elves left, that no one else was hiding in the fortress, and the coast, and the forests. I scoured the kingdom, eager to make sure every fae was safe.

But I was deluding myself. Hiding.

Almost three weeks after we left Masarn, Lennox and I were camped in the middle of the forest after searching it for almost ten hours—we had divided the forest into sections and did one a day.

Lennox turned the squirrel skewered on top of the fire. For days now, I could feel he was holding back something. Every time I asked what was wrong, he snapped at me, saying nothing was wrong.

Finally, that night, he cracked.

He threw a small branch into the fire and got up to his feet. "I'm done with this."

I stared at him from across the fire. I wish I could say I was surprised, but I wasn't. "What do you mean?"

"Being your best friend sucks right now," he said. "I understand things are hard at the capital, but are you really going to do this again? How many years are you planning on hiding this time?" I lowered my gaze to the fire. "I stayed with you. Because I'm your friend, but also because I wanted to make a name for myself. I'm known throughout the kingdom, rust, throughout Wyth because of you, and I'll forever be thankful for that, but I don't want to spend the next decade camping in damp forests and eating critters." He kicked at the fire, sending dirt toward our dinner. I couldn't say I cared. "I want to go back, take my place in the army in the capital, and stay there." He paused. His shoulders sagged a little. "I wish you would join me."

"I can't," I muttered.

Lennox nodded. He let out a sigh. "If you ever need me, I'll be there for you. Goodbye, for now, Red."

He shapeshifted into his fox and disappeared into the night.

When I was alone in the near darkness with a ruined dinner and a quiet forest, I allowed myself to think and feel. For weeks, I had been pushing everything—*everything*—back. Ignoring it all. I wanted to move, to run, to do something, to feel useful and busy so these thoughts and feelings wouldn't find me.

It was time to stop running.

And once I had allowed the thoughts and feelings to come, they didn't stop. A pain started in my chest, a deep hurt that I had been nurturing. Lennox was right. I was a rusting coward. Hiding in this rusting forest while my mate was beside the future king, being roped into a future where I couldn't reach.

No, I couldn't let that happen. I hadn't fought for her hard enough the first time. I couldn't make that same mistake.

I put out the fire, discarded my dinner so an animal could find it, and turned into my fox. The first step was the hardest.

I ran back to the Oren Palace.

I ARRIVED at the palace's front courtyard after two days and nights of running almost nonstop. I was dirty, tired, and sweaty, but I didn't care. Not right now.

Still in my fox form, I crossed the inner gates—the guards recognized me right away—and saw as Lugh led Blair from the palace's entrance to her family's carriage, parked a few feet from the front stairs. He was holding her hand.

A band of jealousy tightened in my chest.

They saw me coming and halted.

Blair dropped Lugh's hand. "Red?" she asked, her gaze incredulous.

I shifted into my fae form and approached them. "I'm late, but I'm here." I reached for Blair and wrapped my hand around her wrist. I pulled her closer to me. "I'm sorry, Lugh. I can't let you marry her. She's my mate."

Around us, the guards and pages and handmaids had gone utterly silent. Even Blair's mother, waiting inside the carriage, was shocked.

"Red—"

"No, let me finish," I interrupted my brother before he could protest. "I've been stupid, trying to ignore my feelings, but I can't anymore. I love Blair. I'm her mate, and I would rather die than see her with someone else. Even if that's you."

Blair wrapped both her arms around mine and rested her chin on my upper arm. "Finally, you've come to your senses."

I stared at her. Then at Lugh. Why wasn't he protesting? Why was she holding on to me without at least explaining things to Lugh? "What's happening?" I asked in a low voice.

Lugh chuckled. "We broke the engagement, you idiot. We haven't announced it yet."

My eyes bugged. "What?"

Lugh explained to me about their conversation, and as his words sank in, my chest felt lighter and lighter. I couldn't help the smile that spread over my lips. I turned to Blair. "Is this true?"

She nodded, her amber eyes sparkling in the sunlight. "It is true." Then, a frown appeared between her brows. She punched me in the shoulder. "But you deserve a beating. You left me again."

"I know, I know." I held both her hands in mine. "I was stupid and feeling guilty. But I was wrong." I tugged her closer and she came, no resistance at all. "But I'm here now, and I'm not leaving unless you tell me to. And even then, I might argue about it."

With a new smile, Blair stepped into me and cupped my face. "Finally."

I leaned into her and rested my forehead on hers. "I love you, Blair. I've loved you since we were younglings, and I didn't even know what love was."

"I love you too, you big stupid rake."

I laughed.

"What? No!" her mother protested from inside the carriage. She leaned closer to the door and pointed her finger at us. "That's unacceptable. Blair, you're betrothed to Prince Lugh. You'll be queen!"

Blair straightened and faced her mother. "Not anymore."

"But ..." Her mother's face fell. "You want to be queen."

"I want to serve the fae of the Autumn Court," Blair said. "I don't need to be a queen for that."

"I've made her an advisor to the crown," Lugh explained. By his smile, he was proud. I was too. "As for you." He glanced at me and the amusement left his face. "I could go on and on about how stupid you are, but I know you weren't yourself the past few weeks." He took a step closer to me. "Let's forget that and move on from here. When we were younger, we discussed you serving as my commander. Then you left. I tried to lead the army, but I can't anymore. Though I'm in good health, I'm still weak and the healer has started to think it's permanent." He let out a sigh. "I need you. I need you to stay here, to be my commander." He glanced at Blair and me. "With the both of you by my side, I'm sure we'll do great things for our kingdom."

I glanced at Blair and she nodded at me. How could I say no to that?

I nodded. "I'll stay."

SIX MONTHS LATER

BLAIR

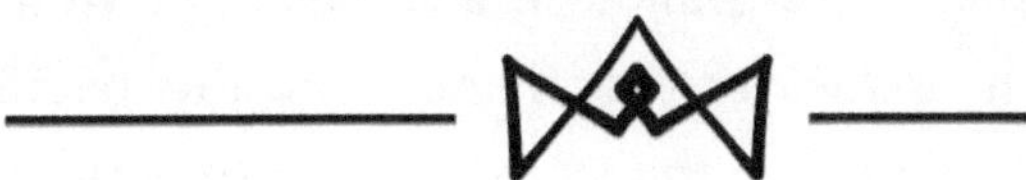

THE CEREMONY COULDN'T HAVE BEEN PRETTIER. If someone asked me, I would say my wedding to Red had been more elegant and happier than Lugh's coronation a couple of months back, but perhaps I was biased.

In the center of the ballroom, Red spun me under his arm, pushing me away for half a second, then he pulled me back to him, holding me tight in his arms. He smiled at me, and I couldn't help smiling back at him. He looked so dashing in a dark brown suit with red embroidery. His face was clean shaven, and his hair had grown. He wore it pulled back in a loose ponytail at his nape.

As for me, I had tried going for a simpler approach to the whole thing, but with Queen Aurelia showing an enthusiasm we hadn't expected from her, and my mother's pampering, I decided to let them dote on me. After all, this was a once-in-a-lifetime deal. I could live with it. But in the end, I fell in love with my elegant white dress and its fine burgundy details and crystals. My red hair had been pulled into an elaborate bun behind my back, with half of it falling down in curls.

The ballroom followed a similar theme with white, brown, and dark red taking over the place. I always thought the place was grandiose and beautiful with its rough wooden archways and chandeliers, the red and orange vines creeping up the walls, and the smooth, dark floors. But with the added tables and their orange and red centerpieces, the rustic wooden chairs, the golden cutlery, the ballroom felt enchanted.

Mahaera had hosted the ceremony and officiated our wedding in a room full of friendly faces, faces that now stood around the dance floor, watching as Red and I danced our first dance as a married couple.

As we spun around, I saw them all. King Cadewyn, Queen Amber, and Princess Chiara, Cade's sister, from the Winter Court. Queen Hayley and General Ashton from the Spring Court. King Varian, Queen Layla, and former Queen Natsia from the Summer Court. Prince Nox and Princess Amaya from the Night Court. King Tenen and Queen Hemera from the Day Court.

We had invited fae from all over Wyth, but some hadn't responded. That was the case of King Altan and Queen Zora from the Dawn Court who, after stepping back when Vasant threatened to destroy the Spring Court, decided to disappear inside their own kingdom. We hadn't heard news from them ever since.

From here, I could also see Willow beside Princess Maize, and Queen Aurelia with them. On her other side stood King Lugh and Gaia, the young librarian he had once fallen in love with. He had found her working in a small village on the border of the kingdom and had offered her a job in the palace's library. She had accepted it right away, and since then, I had seen them walking the palace's courtyards together often. Because he was king, Lugh was courting her slowly and by the book. I wished she was the one for him and they would soon mate. We could use another wedding like this in six months, or a year.

Along with the royal family were my parents, Jora, and Sage. My father looked interested in the event, while my mother and Jora both had handkerchiefs in their hands and frequently wiped at their eyes. Sage looked stoic as ever, though I had seen him sniffling once during the ceremony.

"Did I tell you you look ridiculously gorgeous in that dress?" Red asked, his voice low.

My attention snapped back to him. "No." Yes, he had. Several times. I just liked to hear him say it.

"If this wasn't our party and we were entertaining all these fae, I would whisk you away to our chambers right now." The glint in his eyes grew darker with desire.

A delicious shiver rolled down my spine.

As much as I wanted to leave with him right now, we stayed until the end of the reception. The dance floor opened, our friends and family joined us. Red and I danced with countless fae, we ate scrumptious food, drank a little, chatted with everyone, laughed often, and danced more.

It had been a beautiful and heartwarming day.

Dutiful hosts, Red and I stayed in the ballroom until the last guest left. Then, hand in hand, we walked through the palace's corridors to our chambers. Usually, Sage and Lennox accompanied us wherever we went, but tonight they had not. But they knew that with the many guards stationed along the palace's corridor, there was no need to worry about us.

Red and I entered our new chambers. Red closed the door and turned to me. He held my hands in his and looked into my eyes. "Blair ..." He cleared his throat. "There are no words to describe how I feel right now. I've always loved you, but I never thought this would happen." He squeezed my hands. "I'm the happiest fae alive; I can guarantee you that."

I smiled, my heart full. Red wasn't big on words or feelings. The fact that he wanted to voice this made me proud of him. Of us.

"I love you too, my rebel prince," I whispered. I guided his hands around my waist. "Now shut up, rip this dress off me, and kiss me."

He offered me a lopsided grin. "My pleasure."

Without wasting a second, Red leaned into me and kissed me as his hands traveled to the clasps holding my dress in place. He didn't break the kiss or stop working on my dress as he guided us deeper into our chambers.

Soon, my dress was a pile of fabric at our feet along

with his jacket. We still didn't break the kiss as we both worked to get rid of his tunic and pants. And once it was all gone, Red only pulled back to push me against a wall and kneel in front of me.

"Oh, by the chilly wind," I muttered as he hooked one of my legs over his shoulder and pressed his lips to my core. My knee jerked and I reached to the curtain from the window hanging by my side for balance. I clutched it tight when Red sucked on my clit and slid not one, but two fingers inside me. "Oh," I whispered again, knowing this would be quick. Because I couldn't resist him. Every time Red touched me, it was like he lit me on fire. Being in his arms, in his bed, was the best thing I had ever experienced.

Red knew just how to ignite me. He sucked and licked my clit, hard and long, and he thrust his fingers inside me fast and deep. I felt my muscles tightening, my body seizing. I knew this would be fast. I gasped and broke into a million pieces as the climax took over me. My body went limp, but before I could fall, Red was up and holding me against the wall. And then he hooked my legs around his waist and pushed inside me.

I gasped again as his cock filled me. I came alive again and held on to his shoulders as he drove into me, pushing me against the wall, an onslaught of pleasure I wasn't sure I could take.

"You feel so good," he muttered in my ear. "And you are all mine." He let out a growl before claiming my mouth with his.

Yes, yes, I was all his, forever. I held on to his shoulders as he took me, as he moved in and out, in and out, in a rhythm that made me breathless. By the chilly wind, he was the one who felt so good, so hot. I ran my nails around his shoulders, down his back, grazing the many muscles that contracted with his movements. Red was pure perfection.

All of a sudden, Red dropped my legs and took a step back. I raised my eyebrows at him, but he showed me that wicked half-grin of his as he made a circle with his index finger. I smiled at him as I turned around, bracing my hands on the wall. Red grabbed my waist and entered me from behind. Instantly, my legs trembled. There was something about the position, the way his cock rubbed deep inside me that made me weak.

Red started moving slowly, dragging this out as much as he could. I wasn't complaining. But when he leaned over me and ran his lips over my shoulders and between my shoulder blades, a delicious shiver shook my body, and I wanted more. Now.

"Please, move," I urged him. I reached back and grazed my fingers against his hips.

"What do you want?" he asked in my ear.

"You. Inside me. Faster. Harder. Now," I croaked.

Red obliged. His hands tightened around my waist and he plunged inside me, as fast and hard and deep as I liked. I closed my eyes, letting the pleasure carry me away. This was too much. I wouldn't last long again.

Red slid his hands over my stomach until they both cupped my breasts. He squeezed, pinching the nipples. I cried out. Red groaned. I felt his body tensing right along with mine. He was close too.

"So good," he whispered.

"I know." I started moving with him, meeting him half-way, taking him even deeper and harder. "Oh, rust. Keep going."

He did ... until I cried out as I came. A moment later, Red stilled as the climax shook his body. He wrapped a hand around my waist, leaned his head over my shoulder, and pressed us both against the wall, bracing himself so we wouldn't fall.

When the tremors were gone, Red picked me up in his arms and took me to our bed. "We never made it here," he said with a chuckle. He laid me down in the soft mattress before spreading his beautiful naked body beside mine.

"Well, we'll have time to rectify that."

He raised an eyebrow at me. "You want round two? Give me five minutes and I'm game."

I tapped my wrist. "I'm waiting."

"You're impossible." Red pulled me against him, his arms protectively around me. "And that's one of the many reasons I love you."

I placed my hand over his heart and my chin over his hand, so I could look at him. "I love you too."

He pulled me closer so he could place a quick kiss on my lips. "Welcome to your new life, Princess Blair."

"As long as you're beside me, I'm happy, Prince Redlen."

His eyes locked onto mine. "Forever."

"Forever."

DID you enjoy reading about my sexy fae? Then I bet you'll love reading about my hot vampires. Try *The Vampire Heir* —the first of a series, FREE at all vendors!

THANK YOU

Thank you for reading *Autumn Rebel*!

Reviews are very important for authors. If you liked my book, please consider leaving a review on your favorite online retailer and/or on goodreads, please!

Did you like this book? You can check out other books of mine:

The Midnight Test (Rite World: Lightgrove Witches 1): a clueless witch is invited to join a powerful coven—but only if she aces a difficult test.

The Demon Kiss (Rite World: Blackthorn Hunters Academy book 1): a fast-paced story about a young woman who finds out she's a demon hunter, and the half-demon intent on protecting her against all evil.

The Vampire Heir (Rite World 1: Rite of the Vampire): a dark and mysterious paranormal romance about a vampire and a young woman with a secret.

The Warlock Lord (Rite World 4: Rite of the Warlock): a thrilling and kick-ass paranormal romance about a werewolf and warlock.

Heart Seeker (The Fire Heart Chronicles book 1): an urban fantasy series about a young woman who finds herself at the center of a mysterious supernatural world.

Destiny Gift (The Everlast Series book 1): a post-apocalyptic urban fantasy series about a young woman with a special power that can save the world.

Don't forget to sign up for my Newsletter to find out about new releases, cover reveals, giveaways, and more!

If you want to see exclusive teasers, help me decide on covers, read excerpts, talk about books, etc, join my reader group on Facebook: Juliana's Club!

ABOUT THE AUTHOR

While USA Today Bestselling Author Juliana Haygert dreams of being Wonder Woman, Buffy, or a blood elf shadow priest, she settles for the less exciting—but equally gratifying—life as a wife, a mother, and an author. She resides in North Carolina and spends her days writing about kick-ass heroines and the heroes who drive them crazy.

Subscribe to her mailing list to receive emails of announcement, events, and other fun stuff related to her writing and her books: www.bit.ly/JuHNL

For more information:
www.julianahaygert.com

facebook.com/julianahaygert

twitter.com/julianahaygert

instagram.com/juliana.haygert

goodreads.com/juliana_haygert

pinterest.com/julianahaygert

bookbub.com/authors/juliana-haygert

youtube.com/julianahaygert

ALSO BY JULIANA HAYGERT

To find links and more info, go to:

www.julianahaygert.com/books/

Shorts

Into the Darkest Fire

Standalones

Daughter of Darkness

Rite World: Lightgrove Witches

The Midnight Test (Book 1)

The Midnight Spell (Book 2)

The Midnight Flame (Book 3)

The Midnight Dare (Book 4)

Rite World: Blackthorn Hunters Academy

The Demon Kiss (Book 1)

The Hunter Secret (Book 2)

The Soul Bond (Book 3)

The Shadow Trials (Book 4)

The Infernal Curse (Book 5)

Rite World

The Vampire Heir (Book 1)

The Witch Queen (Book 2)

The Immortal Vow (Book 3)

The Warlock Lord (Book 4)

The Wolf Consort (Book 5)

The Crystal Rose (Book 6)

The Wolf Forsaken (Book 7)

The Fae Bound (Book 8)

The Blood Pact (Book 9)

The Wyth Courts

Winter King (Book 1)

Spring Warrior (Book 2)

Summer Prince (Book 3)

Autumn Rebel (Book 4)

The Fire Heart Chronicles

Heart Seeker (Book 1)

Flame Caster (Book 2)

Sorrow Bringer (Book 3)

Earth Shaker (Novella)

Soul Wanderer (Book 4)

Fate Summoner (Book 5)

War Maiden (Book 6)

The Everlast Series

Destiny Gift (Book 1)

Soul Oath (Book 2)

Cup of Life (Book 3)

Everlasting Circle (Book 4)

Willow Harbor Series

Hunter's Revenge (Book 3)

Siren's Song (Book 5)

Breaking Series

Breaking Free (Book 1)

Breaking Away (Book 2)

Breaking Through (Book 3)

Breaking Down (Book 4)

www.ingramcontent.com/pod-product-compliance
Lightning Source LLC
Chambersburg PA
CBHW021146190726
48288CB00008B/2854